To my dad Clint;
my father-in-law John;
and my best friend Gerald:
three good men who left the world at different times
and different ways, but each one far too soon.
I love you guys, and wish you were all still here.

Montag Press
ISBN: 978-1-940233-18-5
Cover art © 2015 Sebastian J. Gomez
Cover design, layout, & e-book © 2015 Rick Febré

Montag Press Team:
Project Editor – Mara Hodges
Managing Director – Charlie Franco

A Montag Press Book
www.montagpress.com
Montag Press
1066 47th Ave. Unit #9
Oakland CA 94601 USA

Montag Press, the burning book with the hatchet cover, the skewed word mark and the portrayal of the long-suffering fireman mascot are trademarks of Montag Press.

Printed & Digitally Originated in the United States of America
10 9 8 7 6 5 4 3 2 1

IRON AND SMOKE

A NOVEL BY BRANDON NOLTA

MONTAG

IRON AND SMOKE

Prologue

Missouri, 1864

Autumn chill settled on the willow trees with the night, chasing away the last gasps of brutal summer heat with the promise of clouds and snow to come. Despite the bite in the air, the nocturnal life of the Missouri countryside was as active as ever, the hunters and the hunted settling into their eternal roundabout. *Comforting in their way*, thought Simon Moore as he listened at his study window, waiting for darkness to take full hold. His work for the evening was best done by moonlight. Not all of his neighbors held to Missouri's official neutrality in the War Between the States, and some loyalties remained unclear.

Tall and lean, with sharp features softened by a welcoming grin and kind eyes, and deceptively strong from years of labor maintaining his small farm, Simon Moore was a distinctive man in his part of the world. His colleagues in the Western Council frowned on that, he knew; magi—or wizards, as his neighbors might have said—were best served by being unobtrusive. Still, this was his home, a place he'd built through hard work and sacrifice, and this was where he would stay until they threw dirt on him.

You get caught by border ruffians, he thought, *that might be soon.*

"Uncle?" a voice said. A smile played swiftly across Simon's face. The voice's owner was supposed to be in bed, asleep and unaware of his granduncle's activities.

"Aquinas, you're supposed to be in bed," Simon said, attempting his best stern voice as he turned from the window. He drummed his fingers on the ancient text in his hand, feeling the raised pattern of the pentagram on his fingertips. It tingled faintly on his skin, the fundamental symbolism of the shape—five points, corresponding to both the fingers of the hand and the foundational qualities of the classical universe, bound in a circle—drawing an infinitesimal fraction of magical potential to itself simply by existing. The idea of writing a letter to his old scholarly acquaintance James Maxwell and asking how he would explain this in terms of currents and forces flashed across his mind.

"True," his grandnephew said, standing alertly in the doorway. Though only just turned 12, Aquinas Moore was nearly as tall as his granduncle and just as lean. His features still carried a trace of childhood, but Simon could easily see the man to come: solid features, a quick and easy smile, no lack of female attention. He could also see the wild potential in Aquinas, the gift of magic that often flowed through family trees, though it frequently skipped a branch or two. Tragedy had brought Aquinas to Simon, but the loss of his nephew and all his family save Aquinas, in a fire the year before the country fell apart, was balanced by the love and pride Simon felt at seeing Aquinas grow into the man he was becoming. Soon Aquinas would leave home to begin his Council training, and Simon both yearned for and dreaded that day.

"You're going out on the Railroad again," Aquinas said. Simon kept his face still, but his heart sped up a few beats. He'd believed he'd kept his work secret from Aquinas, not because he feared any disapproval from his kin—he'd raised Aquinas better than that—but because he didn't want any suspicion to fall on him should Simon ever be caught. Caution and the judicious use of subtle spellcraft had kept him unnoticed so far, but he wasn't the only magic user around, and luck always ran out eventually.

"Yes," Simon said, seeing no point in denial. His surprise at Aquinas' statement was such that it was another brace of seconds before he noticed Aquinas was fully dressed and carrying a lantern. "Did you want to see me off?"

"I'd like to help, if I can," Aquinas said. "Surely you could use another set of hands, or a lookout."

"I could," Simon said, "but there's a reason I haven't told you about my activities. The Railroad isn't welcome here, and should the ruffians ride by, the night could get unfriendly."

In reply, Aquinas held out his left hand, palm up. From the lantern hanging from his right hand, a spark leaped onto his palm in a liquid, shining arc, spinning slowly over his skin. As Simon watched, the spark sped up, flattening and growing until it resembled a whirling top, spinning bands of light and flame into a sheet of roiling heat. Suddenly, the whirling mass popped, showering sparks and smoke as a thin tongue of flame wrapped around Aquinas' hand, then leaped back into the lantern, leaving only the faint smell of smoke and singed hair. Aquinas shook his hand briefly, as if he was trying to wake it up, but didn't swear.

"So you'll light their lanterns from a distance?" Simon asked. Aquinas started, a flash of pique in his eyes, but said nothing. Simon laughed, his teasing over.

"Sorry. You've clearly been practicing, and I know you can be of help. If you're sure you want to take the risk…"

"You do," Aquinas said.

His granduncle nodded. "It's worth it to me. I'm proud to see it is to you." He walked across the study, footsteps resounding off the book-stuffed shelves, and clapped his closest kin on the shoulder. Simon looked Aquinas in the eye and saw only resolution. The magus nodded and led his grandnephew into the night.

Midnight came and went, and only the waning moon kept Simon and Aquinas company. As they walked toward the pre-arranged meeting place, Simon explained to Aquinas what was to come.

"We'll meet my contact near the crossroads," Simon said as they walked beneath a natural canopy, moonlight speckling their faces through the softly shifting leaves. "Sometimes she has a family with her, sometimes just one or two. We'll make our greetings, exchange news, and take our passengers west, toward the river. From there, another contact will take them by boat to another stop, and so on until freedom. We're too far south to do it ourselves, but at least we can help."

"Do the other contacts know about magic, what you can do?" Aquinas asked.

Simon thought for a minute. "I think the one we'll meet first suspects. It hasn't come up in conversation, though."

A low hooting growl echoed overhead, the full-throated sound of a great horned owl. Simon stopped walking and held a hand up to Aquinas, who stopped and cocked his head upward, listening for the signal he'd been told to expect. The sound paused briefly, followed by a longer growl. Both men waited expectantly for the third call, delivered in a higher pitch as a female owl would.

The third call came, in the same pitch as the first two.

Without conscious thought, Simon reached for his nephew with his left hand, grabbing his upper arm while making a focusing runesign with his right hand. As Aquinas watched, the knife-edged shadows cast by the brilliant white blaze of the moon became fuzzy at the edges, and he understood his granduncle had cast a cloaking glamour. Aquinas opened his mouth to speak, but before he could do so, he heard the nickering of horses spurred to gallop, and knew to keep his silence.

Border ruffians, Aquinas thought, *most likely*. Like most in Missouri, Aquinas was familiar with the stories of anti-abolition raiders, riding from Kansas to Missouri and back, raiding homesteads thought to be pro-free black, attacking abolitionists, and doing their best to frighten people away from Union sympathies. Quantrill's raid of Lawrence, Kansas, the year before was but one of many such attacks, Aquinas knew, by these groups. He also knew the ruffians usually went about heavily armed, and neither he nor Simon had brought a gun. Silently, Aquinas focused his will and began gathering energy to him, hoping that when the time came, he could figure out how to use it effectively without killing.

With the glamour cast, Simon turned to Aquinas and motioned him to follow. They quickly moved off the road and into the trees, taking care to avoid the brush and giving away their position. Seconds later, a group of horsemen rode into view, moonlight revealing the lighter shade of their piecemeal uniforms to be mainly Confederate gray. Toward the back of the group, a wagon with a cage set into it brought up the rear, with two shapes enclosed. Aquinas thought it was a man and a woman, but could not make out details through the darkness and the glamour. He counted seven riders, including the wagon driver.

One rider, taller than the rest on a massive shadowy stallion, raised his hand to bring the group to a halt. As they did so, the rider lifted a thin chain over his head and began swinging it like a lasso, revealing a small bell-shaped censer on the end that spilled, then flung, a dark powder into the night air.

Aquinas looked around, wondering what the point was, when he felt his granduncle draw a sharp breath. Simon pointed at a spot just above them about 10 feet away. Aquinas' eyes followed Simon's finger. At first, he missed what drew Simon's attention, until a tiny flash caught his gaze. Once he knew what to look for, it was unmistakable: sparkles in the air, following the general shape of Simon's hunting glamour. The smell of rust wafted over Aquinas.

"Iron dust," Simon whispered in Aquinas' ear. "Clever."

The rider theatrically sniffed the air. "I believe that's your telltale musk on the breeze, Simon. Do come out from where you're hiding by that tree."

Simon motioned for Aquinas to move behind the tree as Aquinas walked forward. A quick runesign split the glamour in two, one part cleaving tightly to Aquinas, now out of range of the iron dust behind a large box elder. Aquinas watched as the sparks gathered around Simon, drawn in by the additional power he pumped into the spell, until Simon ended it with a sharp gesture and appeared before the ruffians suddenly, visibly surprising all but the tall rider.

"You're some way from home, Belfort. What drove you out of Le Chat Rouge?"

"The only thing that could drive a man like me from New Orleans, Simon: the need for money. I'll thank you to avoid reminding me of all those lovelies I left behind to come up here, chasing after these creatures." Belfort waved one hand nonchalantly at the wagon, its prisoners standing at the iron bars with matching looks of despair. "I suppose you were the next stop for these two."

"Not much point in lying."

"Give it a try. Maybe we'll just burn your farm."

"No wonder you were thrown out of the Council; no

sense of finesse."

Belfort sighed. "Old news, Simon. As are you." He turned to the nearest rider. "Shoot him, and let's get these Negroes back to their owner. I detest Missouri."

"By the Light, Belfort, haven't you ever tried negotiating before? You're terrible at this game," Simon asked, standing calmly in the road, hands behind his back, as if getting shot happened every day. Only Aquinas could see his granduncle's quick, precise signing, too fast for Aquinas to read. Belfort, however, was not fooled.

"Now, damn your eyes," Belfort yelled to his underling, a squat lump wearing a torn officer's jacket. One smooth motion brought the man's service revolver to bear on Simon, and Aquinas realized that the ruffian could cock the hammer and fire before Simon finished his cast, which Aquinas suspected would be some kind of flora-based spell, his uncle's strongest specialty.

Without thinking, Aquinas summoned his gathered power and will, focused on the rider pointing a gun at his granduncle, and released a half-visualized burst of power, designed to make the thuggish gunman release the gun as if he'd been stung. Instead, a ball of spitting lightning arced through the night, flash-frying the gunman's hand in a sizzle of electricity and burned flesh. The revolver flew from the hand of the now-screaming gunman, who instantly cradled the scorched appendage to his chest, and struck another rider solidly in the head. As the stunned rider fell, Belfort opened his mouth, but before the Cajun magus could speak, Simon finished his rune casting, raised both hands into the air, and shouted a word in an ancient tongue Aquinas didn't recognize.

The trees roared. For some time afterward, Aquinas would occasionally have nightmares about that moment. In sleep, he would again hear the slow groaning of wood up-rooting from the earth; the whip and crack as branches swung through the air to grab the ruffians and throw them, keening, into the sky or shake them back and forth as a dog shakes a bone; and the deep bone-grinding bellow of enraged titans striking, sometimes cutting, into flesh and blood. Even as he remembered that magically—miraculously—none of the ruf-fians died that night, and that even the Cajun who led the gang was captured and delivered to the law alive, his memories in-sisted on replaying the damage they suffered before that. His nightmares showed him every broken limb, every flay mark, every bruise. Worst of all, he remembered clearly the largest of the trees, a mighty red maple with roots like tentacles, grab-bing the Cajun, Belfort, and swiftly tearing his tongue from his mouth, spraying blood and a smattering of teeth into the night.

"It needed to be done," Simon told Aquinas, after they had freed the couple from the cage and loaded the broken and bleeding ruffians into it. "Belfort is a voxumancer; his magic is based not just in words, but in his voice. Once he heals, he'll be able to use basic magic, even without a tongue."

"Wouldn't a gag have worked just as well?" Aquinas asked.

"I once saw him clear a ship of rats just by humming," Si-mon said. "What might he call out of these woods on us, if giv-en the chance? In any case, if we hadn't done so, the Council would have as soon as he was in custody. Maybe if he reforms, they'll let a Roddy grow it back for him in a few decades."

Dawn was edging over the trees before Simon and Aqui-nas reached their homestead, after leaving the wounded pris-oners safely housed in the town jail, watched over by the local sheriff and a deputy with a low-level Council rating. Neither had spoken on the journey home. For his part, Simon wondered if he'd erred in allowing Aquinas to come along. What he'd seen was brutal, but by magi logic, necessary. The Council might have done worse, and many of those in it might not have taken such care to preserve the lives of the other ruffians, Simon knew, even though protecting life was one of the Council's highest principles.

"Aquinas, please know that what you saw tonight wasn't representative of being magi," Simon said as they reached the broad deck of the front porch. Aquinas stopped on the step and looked his uncle in the eye. "There are many wonders in this world, and—"

"Uncle," Aquinas interrupted, "I know what you're going to say. You don't need to apologize or persuade."

"Even so," Simon said.

Aquinas smiled and held out his hand. A spark hung in the air over his skin, floating and lazily revolving. Simon watched it for a second, seeing it spin slowly, stop, and reverse direction.

"I am magi, like you," Aquinas said, "and I want to know more."

Simon smiled as the day began to break around him.

"You will."

Chapter 1

Western United States, 20 years later

Sunrise spilled quickly over the barren lands, running over patches of green and crabbed hills like quicksilver from a flask. The light crept up the dirtied window of the Pullman car, lighting the tall, quiet passenger within. From childhood, the Western lands fascinated Aquinas Moore; every chance he found, he climbed the mighty apple tree outside his granduncle's farmstead home and imagined himself heading into new lands, exploring the frontier, replaying the stories he heard and read in his mind. Dreams of unexplored lands and unmade spaces on the map drew him, firing his reveries as he grew into a young man, learning the mystical and mundane forces behind men's actions. Even now, with skills and burdens he never imagined as a child, being in the land he'd spent many nights dreaming about on Uncle Simon's wild Missouri homestead thrilled a deep corner of his heart.

Without thinking, he laid his right arm across the sill of the open window beside him. Before he could lean out and catch a breath of air not tainted with coal smoke, he felt a shiver of repulsion in his bones from the iron embedded in the window frame. He snatched his arm back, unhurt but *warned* somehow, as if he'd spotted a fat summer wasp from the corner of his eye. It had been a long trip, and he'd momentarily forgotten the nearness of ferrous metal; the car was mostly wood and brass. Railroads saved their iron for tracks and engines and wheels, the only comforting aspect of a train ride for natural magi like Aquinas.

Quickly the shiver faded, but the stirrings of his good mood fled with it. Had the diplomatic packet at his side, the reason for his journey, been a little more urgent, the Council probably would have sent him via dreamwalking or even, Light preserve him, a flight spell of some kind. Like everyone else in his chapter, he'd heard the longstanding rumor about the Boston chapter head having a Persian rug with a levitation spell tied into every individual knot, a fantastic investment in power that could keep the tapestry aloft probably until the Last Trump. Not that a low-level envoy, even a capable magus like Aquinas, would get to use it for any reason.

No point in bitterness, he told himself, missing his Uncle Simon, dead for fifteen years but still clear in his thoughts. Aquinas wished his granduncle's reassuring wisdom was available on this issue. Meeting with the individual tribes of the Indian nations was never easy to arrange, but an audience with Calls Thunder Song, the only living shaman capable enough and in high enough esteem with the Spirit Councils to hold lodge…it took nearly two years of negotiation to arrange, and he was only delivering a report. Aquinas knew his strengths, and the fine and subtle art of shamanistic diplomacy wasn't among them. If he was lucky, Calls Thunder Song might deign to accept the packet while awake.

Out the window, the front of the iron snake in which he rode curved south, pulling slowly toward a dark smudge on the earth. Aquinas mentally consulted the schedule he'd memorized last night over strong coffee and hard biscuits; the town before him was Copper Line, two stops before his destination. An hour's layover was scheduled, long enough to seek a breakfast more filling than Pullman rations, Aquinas hoped. Unlike other magi he studied with during his formal education period,

Aquinas could eat whatever he damn well wished. He watched the smudge grow ever closer and thought longingly of bacon and a well-turned egg. Something about the vast sky and empty earth gave him a ferocious appetite.

As if summoned, a porter materialized at his elbow. "Coffee, sir? Maybe a biscuit?" A plate of potential skeet targets rested on the tray in the porter's powerful arms, a small dish of wan butter perched to the side. A shined tin coffee pot, painted gold with red trim, steamed next to a stack of clean white cups, too dainty for train rides but miraculously unchipped all the same. Aquinas took a cup and shook his head at the biscuits. The porter smiled and deftly poured a steaming draft of coffee.

"There'll be breakfast at the station diner, sir. It won't be fancy or cheap, but you'll leave your hunger there."

"Fine with me," Aquinas said, surprised by the porter's poetic turn of phrase. "We'll be stopped an hour?"

"Yes, sir. Train leaves the station at 9:05 on the minute. You won't want to miss it; you can telegraph from there, but the only place to sleep will be the bench, and they're awfully hard come midnight."

"I'll keep that in mind," Aquinas promised. The first sip of coffee hit his mouth, and judging from the searing blast of heat, stripped the enamel from his teeth. He quickly swallowed to keep the roof of his mouth and his tongue from the same scorching.

Nodding, the porter turned away to continue his rounds. An impulse struck Aquinas as he watched the porter, smiling and agile as he poured coffee and handed out biscuits down the aisle, and he opened his Sight for a moment, allowing the illusions of human reality to fall away. He didn't expect to See much; out here, unless a hunting glamour was being used, all a magus could expect to See were the meridians in the earth, pulsing in time with fire and gravity. To see the ley lines of the sky required detailed Seeing, not to mention a dark night. Air magic was strong, but thin as mist even to Seeing eyes. A moderately bright moon easily drowned out the ley lines' iridescences.

The Seeing opened, blossoming another layer of color and motion onto the world. Aquinas, whose natural ability with the Sight was further honed by years of expert training, was dumbstruck by the porter's pyrotechnic aura. It glittered with veins of white and molten blue, fiery in the still air above the passengers, none of whom possessed anything more than the muted red and brown auras of whatever Divine spark granted them souls. His own aura, he knew, was shot through with braided green-and-orange flares, reflecting his natural skill and status as a person whose blood ran strong with magic, and whose family had for generations. The porter, though, was something different. Whatever skills or spells Aquinas learned to do, or might learn to do in his expectedly long life, he would always be fundamentally human. If the porter's aura was any indication, he couldn't say the same.

Without pausing in his spiel, the porter turned toward Aquinas and gave him a short, subtle wink. Brilliant white teeth shone in his smile, and then the porter was facing away, selling another customer on the joys of coffee and biscuits. Around him, the flames of the strongest aura Aquinas had seen, a spicy and brilliant flare of power, danced merrily on the walls and ceiling of the Pullman car.

Aquinas ended the Seeing with a flicker of focused will and wondered who or what he was, how he could stand being close to so much iron, and why such a being would choose to work as a porter. Such power could bring a being many rewards and joys, Aquinas thought. In a way, Aquinas knew

he envied the porter this power; more importantly, the awareness of the power the porter subtly showed. For as long as he
could recall, Aquinas suspected he had gifts unlike those of
others, and soon enough, others more qualified to make that
judgment agreed. Furthermore, his Uncle Simon—unusually
for the time and place—was well steeped in knowledge, magic
and the possibilities of both, and so never kept Aquinas from
learning or studying. However, despite being accepted for
training within the Council's standard time frame, he started
his schooling relatively late, more so than his peers. As a result, Aquinas never quite shook the suspicion he missed a few
things in his schooling, some subtle trick or insight that made
all the laws and knowledge he'd gained fall into place and
present a swirling, lockstep cosmos he could understand. Despite years of study, that understanding he craved hadn't come
to him yet.

One thing, however, was clear to Aquinas: whatever
power the porter wielded or was made from, there was no mal-
ice in it. Something with that much force, that much energy
welded to a corporeal frame probably noted Aquinas as soon
as he climbed onboard in St. Louis, and had taken no action
against him when it would have been easy to do. It was a puz-
zle, but a benign one, and Aquinas had more pressing matters
to consider. Breakfast, the most obvious one, but as the train
began the long process of slowing as it approached Copper
Line, Utah, it was the sealed report in his spell-warded valise
that occupied his thoughts.

His orders from the Council were clear: he was not to
open the report until he reached the camp outside the Shoshone hunting grounds. Aquinas was unsure of the ultimate
reason for his visit, but if Calls Thunder Song—a legendary
shaman who was rumored to have once won a mystical gift in

a bet with Coyote—was asking the Council for help, it wasn't likely to be good. Complicating matters was the fact the Council had declined to use any pressure, sorcerous or otherwise, in the long attrition the U.S. government was fighting against the Indians as a whole. To ask for help in the face of that political affront was unimaginable to Aquinas, and for the first time since he'd received his orders, he wondered if perhaps he didn't want to know.

Too late for second thoughts, Uncle Simon's voice chuckled at him from the depths of memory, and Aquinas conceded the point. The train was noticeably slower now, and the station, grey planks of unpainted wood shoved together in a roughly shack-like shape, was drawing them in like the moon summons the tide. A barely-there tinge of frying bacon and potatoes reached him, and smiling at the thought of breakfast, he tucked the brass-clasped valise under his arm and prepared to stand and stretch. Heavily, the bound report shifted in its case, as if awakening from a long slumber, struggling to be opened and pour out whatever information, whatever secrets it kept within.

Chapter 2

Oaken doors like massive tablets swung open at the lieutenant's approach, gliding silently on well-oiled hinges. The lieutenant, a spit-and-polish West Point graduate named Anderson Caldwell, hadn't seen anyone or anything move, a trick that seemed a little ominous. Still, it wasn't like he was walking into the House of Usher, he told himself. Mr. Pineville's office wasn't in the White House or part of the President's Cabinet, or even near somebody who worked in the Cabinet, but all power starts somewhere. Mr. Pineville's office felt like one of those places.

Caldwell smartly doffed his cap as he stepped inside, his stride brisk and precise as he reached the massive desk in the exact center of the office. A crisp green carpet muffled his steps, and Caldwell idly noted the beautiful but unusual markings and pictures worked into the carpet's surface. Unusual, but Caldwell thought of Mr. Pineville as a man of the world, as did the Washington gossip line, and men of the world often find strange and rare pieces of it to bring back home. Out of habit, he saluted as he stopped.

"No need to salute, Lieutenant," the trim gentleman at the desk said, eyes intent on the newspapers arrayed across the polished hardwood surface. A pair of gold-rimmed spectacles sat at the tip of Mr. Pineville's patrician nose. The glasses were the only thing shiny about Mr. Pineville, who as far as the lieutenant knew always dressed in clean and pressed shades of brown. Looking at Mr. Pineville for very long, Lt. Caldwell found, was like trying to find a black cat on a moonless night: the eyes tended to slide off and lose focus. Caldwell suspected that was a useful trait in politics.

"Sorry, Mr. Pineville," Caldwell said. "Force of habit."

Pineville looked up from his reading. Behind the lenses of his glasses, Pineville's eyes regarded Caldwell with no more interest than if he were a fly buzzing in a window. The official's flat gaze bothered Caldwell for the first few weeks of his tour in Washington, but Pineville had a lot to teach, and Caldwell was learning more than he thought possible about railroads and engineering surveys. He was even considering a transfer to the Army Corps of Engineers.

Slick from humidity and sweat, the bundle under Caldwell's arm slipped, and he remembered the reason for his visit. He handed the bundle to Pineville, who accepted it soundlessly and began to read its contents. "Here are the latest maps and reports from the cavalry and the railroad crews, sir. The crews are making excellent progress. The spur to Windy Falls should be completed by mid-October."

The official said nothing, reading the maps and handwritten reports closely, eyes drinking in every scrap of detail. He pointed to a blank section of the map, where rivers and territory lines ran in great inky loops but no tracks were seen. "What about here?"

Caldwell craned his head to read over the area. "That's Indian allotment land, sir. Southern Paiute, I believe. Union Pacific intends to take the line from Pocatello through here," the lieutenant said, pointing at another region of the map.

Pineville smiled, a dry curve in the bland expanse of his face. "I meant troubles with the Indians, Lieutenant. I understand there have been a few incidents in that area."

"Yes, sir, but the Tenth is there now under Colonel McAlister. He's dealt with Indian troubles before."

Pineville leaned back in his chair. "Yes, I'm sure he has. Tends to raze whole villages, if I remember. At least he did when he was killing Greycoats in Tennessee. I doubt a few Paiute or Shoshone would trouble him any."

Caldwell said nothing. Not only did he not wish to speak ill of a superior officer to a civilian, he wasn't certain Pineville was talking to him anyway. Conversations with the undersecretary sometimes seemed to include presences in the walls, judging by the way Pineville sometimes shifted his head and gazed into empty corners when talking. The lieutenant never actually heard Pineville address someone who wasn't there, but the lieutenant's instincts told him he and Pineville mightn't always agree on what was or wasn't there. Lieutenant Caldwell was wise enough to believe his instincts despite his youth.

The papers rustled as Pineville picked them up again and quickly finished reading through the reports. Caldwell waited patiently; he knew Pineville had a few additions to make, and a few more instructions on the side project only Pineville seemed to know anything about. Caldwell thought it odd at first when the nondescript official began issuing orders for a secondary line to be built off the main Union Pacific line, but with the number of settlers still taking Horace Greeley's forty-year-old advice to go west, it made sense to plan ahead. *Besides,* the lieutenant thought, *however much I've learned, Pineville knows still more, and I doubt I can see the full scope yet.*

Caldwell looked out the large French doors leading to a small balcony overlooking Jefferson Avenue and the daily bustle. The view was of nothing but buildings and sweating people, but occasionally a breeze from the Potomac reached the office, and any relief from the heat was welcome. The lieutenant adjusted his collar and wished the window was open

now. A scattering of grey clouds overhung the building, block-
ing the summer sun briefly. *Some rain to break the heat*, Caldwell thought, a little tag of hope making the thought into a
question.

The sound of stamping drew Caldwell's attention again.
The undersecretary, finished with his perusal and note-taking,
applied his official stamp to a map with new notes and coordinates boldly scratched in pencil. He swiftly rolled the doc-
uments into a tube and handed the bundle to the lieutenant.
"Have the crew chief start work on the Rockhill spur immediately, and send word to McAlister that he is to begin moving
his forces to the northwest."

"How far, sir?"

"Tell him to stop just before he gets attacked and wait. I'll
have new orders for him in a week."

"Yes, sir," the lieutenant said, remembering not to salute
and wondering how to translate Pineville's peculiar phrasing
into orders. He bowed his head, turned and strode sharply out
the door, wondering as he left how those great damned doors
opened so smoothly without anyone pushing them. *It must be
a pulley system*, Caldwell decided.

As the doors shut behind the lieutenant, the undersecretary everyone in the building knew as Mr. Pineville sighed
and leaned back in his chair, rubbing his temples tiredly. By
the First, what an immense effort to actually have to talk to
that damned lieutenant, instead of just yanking him by the soul
and making him do what he was supposed to do, like a great
big sock puppet with a fancy uniform and the power of speech.
Pineville looked up at the ceiling, acknowledging some flurry
in the air, a ripple in the humid heat.

"Things were easier before bureaucracy," he said quietly.

Nothing answered him, and after a moment of quietly

gazing upward, Pineville shook himself and got back to work. With a sequence of staccato taps on a pair of hidden buttons, a secret drawer popped out from underneath the sliding writing shelf. Pineville knew secret drawers were passé for a desk of this size and style, but he was, among other things, a fan of the classics. Carefully, he withdrew a large scroll from the drawer's depths, unrolling the supple vellum on his desk with anticipation. The scroll unfurled to reveal a large, very detailed map of the area where the railroads were building the newest tracks, spread across four states and two territories, rendered in a deep set of colors that would astound anyone who saw them.

In the center of the map, a large area was bounded in lines of forest green, surrounded on all sides by the inked-in press of settlers and cavalrymen. Moving outward, Pineville could see the projected lines of railroad tracks in black, moving closer to becoming real train lines day by day, coming closer to fruition with every swing of the hammer, every driven spike. As he usually did, Pineville traced the lines on the map, watching the colors shift and squirm under the cold ley fire in his fingertips as he followed the routes of his dreams around the green. Angles and lines and iron, making geometric stains on the earth, nothing but a cosmic coincidence.

Until one adds McAlister to the mix, a voice completely different from the voice he used with Caldwell whispered in Pineville's head. *Then a whole new geometry will rise.* His fingers, moving with urges of their own, caressed the vellum, circling around then through the green shaded area until the tip of his index finger came to rest against a dot on the map, a single tiny town called Violet Falls. *Here is where the world will begin again,* Pineville's true voice whispered. *In time.*

Pineville looked up at the ceiling. The smile on his face now was far more real than his usual, and it had teeth. Far too

many for an undersecretary, Lt. Caldwell would have undoubtedly thought, had he been unlucky enough to see it.

"Not soon enough," Pineville said to whatever he saw
above him. "Not nearly soon enough."

Underneath his hand, the shifting colors of the map trembled at his words.

Chapter 3

That porter was right, Aquinas thought as the waitress, stout and weathered as the building where he sat, took away his empty plates and cup. *My hunger is definitely gone.* He sat back in his chair with a contented sigh, stretching his lean arms and considerable length of legs as he did. Uncle Simon used to joke any boots Aquinas wore were seven-league boots, and the magus wished that statement was true. Pullman cars were decent accommodations for a day, but any romance he'd harbored about transcontinental train travel had long vanished. Still, he had only another day of travel to look forward to before reaching his destination; no point in complaining now that he was nearly there.

A few coins paid his bill, and he strode out onto the platform to pass the few minutes until the train left again. Morning was still cool, but summer's dry crackling heat was already building in the air, and another blistering day was expected. Aquinas glanced at the clouds and the ripple of natural energy around them. Sky patterns were unmistakable: rain was many days and many miles away.

From his left, a husky voice said something in a liquid, musical tongue. Aquinas turned to see a compact Indian man standing beside him, dressed in faded cotton clothes and a leather duster the color of storm clouds. A knife of sharpened bone lay low on the Indian's right hip, beaded leather wrapped tight on the hilt. His eyes, Aquinas saw, were light grey, almost silver in color, and something in his bearing suggested a man used to fighting. The wide-brimmed hat perched above a shock of thick black hair was a cowpuncher's chapeau, but the hatband was pure aboriginal American, and Aquinas—who just managed to conceal his startlement at being approached so closely without notice—was not surprised to see a shaman's sigil woven into the colored pictographs. Here was the man he'd been told to meet, six towns and a day sooner than expected.

"Hainch ki-tum-ar-g," Aquinas said in passable Paiute. "Aquinas Moore, magus of the eighth level and special representative of the Western Council, North American branch."

The Indian raised an eyebrow a quarter-inch or so. "English is fine, Mr. Moore. You speak pretty good Paiute. Lucky for you, I'm one of the smart Shoshones who understand it."

Aquinas smiled. *Use tact*, a memory of Uncle Simon's voice whispered, *until you can find a hammer*. "Fortunately, my English is better than my Paiute, sir." He held out his hand, palm up, in the traditional magi handclasp. "Are you Fights the Wind?"

"Today I am," the Indian replied, his eyes and voice flat. Aquinas' hand hung in space for a long second before the shaman reluctantly clasped hands and shook Aquinas' arm sharply twice. It did not surprise Aquinas that Fights the Wind knew Council decorum—despite the long and deplorable history between the white people and the aboriginals, magi from both groups had been in contact since the early 16th century—but it was disquieting to see a diplomatic envoy so unconcerned with the usual niceties, even given the situation.

"Better get your money back from the railroad, Mr. Moore," Fights the Wind said as Aquinas reclaimed his hand from the Indian's firm but noncommittal grip. "You won't need their services for the rest of your trip."

Relief must have shown on his face, because Fights the Wind's eyebrow rose again. Aquinas nodded cordially and excused himself to make the arrangements. He followed the shaman off the platform into the dust of Copper Line's only road after securing a refund for his unused ticket, and walked unhurriedly a pace behind and to the left of his guide, showing the proper deference per Council protocol. Copper Line wasn't much of a town yet, with only a handful of buildings and houses scattered along both sides of the river of dust and horse offal that served as a street, but it took a couple of minutes to pass through at Fights the Wind's leisurely pace. Aquinas had no worries about luggage; other than the diplomatic valise now slung over his shoulder, he had none. Most magi carried everything they needed on their persons, and with the right manipulation of spells and geometric calculation, could carry far more than the average pack mule.

As Aquinas and Fights the Wind crested a small rise on the far side of the livery stable and began walking down the other side, it struck Aquinas that there was no more town to walk through, an impressive amount of open and empty land before them, and no horses in sight. He looked at Fights the Wind, who kept his eyes on the horizon and didn't acknowledge Aquinas' unspoken question. Magi are trained to deal with the unexpected as a matter of course, but taking a stroll through open prairie while still a day's train ride from one's destination sounded more like a trap.

Curious, Aquinas thought, imagining his Uncle Simon questioning the sudden turn the day had taken. *Why aren't I worried about this?*

Aquinas pondered that while he followed Fights the Wind into the western plains, and Uncle Simon's voice calmly explained all that was wrong with the present situation. *The envoy is obviously not concerned with diplomacy, the routine has been changed with no explanation, and you are rapidly walking away from civilization with a possibly hostile shaman of unknown ability: this is probably not going to end with cake*, his dead granduncle's voice told him. *Yet here you walk without a care in the world.*

I know, Aquinas thought. *You're right, but something about this feels…natural. It's not what I expected, but I don't believe it's wrong. I…trust this shaman.*

Enough to just walk into the desert? Simon's voice sounded less amused. *What if he attacks you?*

Aquinas looked at Fights the Wind, casually walking as if he were headed to the mercantile. His hands hung loosely at his sides, and though he never looked at Aquinas, his gaze never moved far from him. Relaxed or not, the shaman gave the impression of an animal preparing to leap, coiled potential energy stored in compact muscles. First attacks were usually magical, but the knife at the shaman's hip looked well-used, and Aquinas didn't doubt his guide had combat experience.

I expect him to, Aquinas thought. *Any time now.*

The magus and the shaman walked in silence for several minutes, following the curve of the land into a wide gully with a shoe's width of creek still flowing through it. In his pocket, the crystalline vibration of his watch told Aquinas it was eleven o'clock, but the heat was already as great as the most blazing summer day in St. Louis. Past a sharp turn to the northeast, the gully opened into what was once the bed of a mighty river, now patched with browning tufts of weeds and scrub brush, with barely enough green in stripes and swaths to make the land look alive. Fights the Wind slowed his pace, and Aquinas stopped to wait for his guide's next move.

The shaman stopped roughly ten paces from Aquinas

and turned slowly as if he had just thought of something to say. Aquinas kept his posture friendly, but made sure his hands were loose and ready. Out of habit, Aquinas opened his Sight and casually glanced around the area, then back at the shaman. As he'd suspected, a meridian ran underneath the ground, and a breath of cool sensation against his Sight told him a ley line was somewhere overhead, available to any magus, shaman or mystical creature.

Fights the Wind looked at him for a long moment, his clear silver eyes giving away no thought or emotion. Aquinas, patient in his skills and training, kept himself calm and relaxed; he was fully aware that tension in the face of uncertainty might be helpful, but it could get him killed just as easily.

"I can't trust you, Aquinas Moore," Fights the Wind finally said, his voice soft but strong in the desert air. "There is something black moving in the world, something pointed at my people."

"Is that why Calls Thunder Song asked for help?"

Fights the Wind shook his head, eyes never leaving Aquinas. "He wasn't asking for help. He believes the whites are responsible for setting this thing upon my people, and the other tribes as well. It's likely not all of you know about it; this evil is too grand even for you butchers to unleash. Still, it rightfully falls to your people to help stop it. He was testing to see how far this black influence has spread."

"How will whatever you're planning to do here help?"

Fights the Wind nodded. "I must find out who you really are, whether you are here to help my people or further the blackness. There are several ways to discover this." Carefully, the shaman reached down with his left hand and undid the clasp on his bone knife. Crackling sounds broke like surf against Aquinas' magus-tuned hearing, the sounds of energy

gathering in the spaces of a shaman's will. "This is the most…
direct."

The idea of a magical duel being more direct than its alternatives left Aquinas simultaneously amused and cold. "Well, then. I accept your challenge in the spirit of its intention."

Fights the Wind nodded again and held his right hand up at eye level, palm out, fingers cupped slightly as if he were holding an invisible ball. Aquinas recognized it as a native gesture of respect; variants of this movement were the first part of a duel between true magi of any stripe. Aquinas matched the shaman's posture and gesture, his jet-green eyes meeting the shaman's silvered gaze. "What is it we fight to?"

The shaman smiled. "Until the answer is clear."

Aquinas thought for a moment, and signaled his agreement with a nod. "I accept your terms."

Fights the Wind squared his shoulders, his expression now as flat as his eyes. The magi shifted into the ceremonial postures, bowed to each other and entered a defensive stance. Each man counted the seconds silently. At three, the duel would begin.

Three, the memory of Uncle Simon's voice said, and in the same instant, Fights the Wind blurred into motion, speaking a thorny phrase in Shoshone as he gestured swiftly with his bone knife, moving far faster than Aquinas believed possible. A defensive ward shaped itself to the magus' will, entangling the serpentine shadow of a curse within its beams, but Fights the Wind was already casting the next attack, tossing a yellow powder into the air and spitting syllables as fast as his mouth could form them. Before the sulfurous powder finished its arc, scorpions were forming and falling softly to the hardpan like rain, chittering as they scuttled poisonously toward Aquinas.

Aquinas usually preferred visualizing his spells, but

he was not above using runes or established magic terms to focus his energy. He raised his left hand in a warding stance and shouted in Latin, calling fire forth from the earth. Sheets of flame erupted from the hardpan, following the arc of his hand as he scorched the shaman's scorpions into cinders. His eyes were on the ground, searching for any stingers the flames missed, but his Sight was on Fights the Wind. An aura flickered over the fire, the deep violet and white of a shaman bound to spirits of earth and sky, and his right hand cast a complex runesign before a conscious thought could form.

Blue and glowing, the runesign materialized over Fights the Wind and unfolded into a brilliant diamond vortex that expanded as the shaman looked up into the clouds. Wind, fierce and roaring, slammed into the shaman and lifted him bodily into the air, spinning wildly as the vortex grew, quickly reaching tornado size. In answer, a blue spark leapt from the vortex, seeming to hang outside the reach of the monstrous wind. Aquinas formed a ward around him, but just as he closed the circle, an answering spark arced from the upper curve of his protection to the blue spark hanging against the cloud-darkened sky, and even before the flash, he realized the clever trap Fights the Wind had loosed on him.

"Oh, hell," Aquinas said as he leapt from the ward's protection. The sparks had been magical potentials; just like electricity, magic had a way of shifting from one pole to another. In a searing flash, a bolt of transferred magical potential drew down the energy of the vortex into Aquinas' ward, turning it into a charring blast of power. Aquinas squeezed his eyes shut to protect them, but the thundering hammerblow of sound tossed him across the gully, ringing his ears and slamming him into the desert floor hard enough to scatter his wits and his breath. He opened his eyes in time to see Fights the Wind fall heavily to the ground, the impact knocking his breath away like the thunder had done to Aquinas.

Carefully, Aquinas got to his feet, swaying as he did but managing to stay balanced. *That could have burned me to charcoal*, Aquinas thought as he shook his head, trying to clear the ringing dizziness from his brain. Fights the Wind (*he's earned that name now*, Aquinas thought) was on his feet, swaying a little like Aquinas, but his eyes were clear. *What now*, Aquinas wondered, but his hands were already in motion, the left acting as a focus while the right cast a runesign, and he roared the ancient name for water, still barely able to hear his own voice.

A puzzled look shadowed Fights the Wind's face, and in his hesitation, the tiny creek in the gully's bottom exploded into fury, brackish water spewing from the earth like lava. Within a heartbeat, a massive sphere of water slammed into place around the shaman, carrying him off the ground and encasing him three feet beyond his arm's reach. The ball floated on a pressurized spume from the creek, keeping Fights the Wind out of reach from the earth and sky, the homes of his gods and the sources of his power.

Fights the Wind's face turned dark with fury and lack of air, and Aquinas could see the shaman's agile hands casting runesigns, but he knew he'd caught his opponent in the right trap. Water was not an element a shaman of earth and sky could use easily; it was too fluid for earth magic and too unmoving for sky workings. Casting runesigns while immersed was something even water witches didn't do, and running out of breath couldn't do much for the focus of will needed. Still dizzy from the thunderbolt, Aquinas slowly understood he'd won the duel, and all he needed now was the acknowledgement.

Hands unencumbered by water motioned, and the ball rumbled closer to Aquinas, close enough he could drink from its surface if he wished. He locked eyes with Fights the Wind, the shaman's face turning a dangerous shade within the watery shell. "Yield?"

The shaman's eyes flashed angrily, but he nodded. His left hand made the runesign for acquiescence, the right hand holding its power in check. Aquinas noted the bone knife was still unclasped, and hoped his sense that Fights the Wind was a man of honor was correct. The magus released the molten core of will that kept the water trapped, and a flood fell to earth, crumbling the dirt he stood on and knocking him off his feet. As he raised his head, he saw the shaman lying on his back six feet away, still and unmoving but for the rise and fall of his chest.

Aquinas sat up, splashing mud and dirty water, and used his Sight to check on his opponent. His aura was muted, but still strong; clearly he hadn't drowned, and despite his obvious anger, Aquinas thought the fight was pretty much done for now.

Suddenly the shaman sat straight up in his puddle and looked at Aquinas, water pattering off his hat and coat. Fights the Wind stared at Aquinas for several seconds, long enough to make the magus nervously consider gathering his will for another round, and smiled, a brilliant flash of teeth that seemed to take ten years off the shaman's face.

"You're a clever son of a bitch, Mr. Moore."

Aquinas laughed and, getting to his feet, offered Fights the Wind his hand.

Chapter 4

asleep in the sky
the thunderbird floats in moonlight baths
stars in its feathers, sun in its talons
dreaming of the night
and wagers over carved bone

Shivers passed around the circle of men seated at the lodge fire as the last few notes of the ancient song trilled and faded into silence. Every man at the circle had heard the song as many times as there were stars in the sky, but Many Voices made it new every time. The elders valued that skill, and so valued Many Voices, even though his mother had been white.

"It sounds better in Paiute," a grumpy voice said from the shadows to the right of Calls Thunder Song. The others, including Many Voices, laughed at this. Decades ago, a party of Quebecois traders on their way to El Paso tangled with the voice's owner, giving him the name of Loup-Garou in terror after fighting with him under the full moon, and he had been irritable ever since, mainly because Calls Thunder Song, delighted with his friend's new name, addressed him only as Loup-Garou from then on. It had been so many years since that legendary battle, and such was Calls Thunder Song's influence even then, only a tiny handful of the tribe knew what Loup-Garou's birth name was. Calls Thunder Song long ago promised himself he would never tell anyone.

"Everything does to you, Loup-Garou," Calls Thunder Song said, to more laughter. "Except your wife."

Loup-Garou made a noise like a buffalo snoring, sharp and disdainful, and settled further into his seat against the rough lodge logs. A knot popped in the fire, showering sparks into the air and casting tiny bursts of light onto Loup-Garou's stony visage, marked by age and a gnarled scar that ran parallel to his nose, ending just above his lip. The same trader that gave him his name also gave him the scar, just before Loup-Garou hacked off a large part of the trader's forearm with his hatchet.

"No language is suitable for her," Loup-Garou agreed. He turned to the other elders, all of whom had known Loup-Garou the better part of twenty years and were well aware of his feelings about his name. The laughter tapered off, and Calls Thunder Song began to speak.

"I have conferred with my son in the dream walking, and I've seen this magus the Council has sent us to report. He doesn't know of the blackness arrayed against us. I believe he is sincere and ready to help."

"They send us a stripling," said White Hawk, a smoke-stained and battle-scarred warrior who was the only person for several days' ride older than Calls Thunder Song, "when we need an oak. I don't see how this magus can be of much help. Is he powerful?"

"Not as much as he will be," Calls Thunder Song said, "but enough to be of some use."

"And what of the news he brings?" said Mangas, the youngest of the elders. Streaks of black still ran in his hair, thick and braided down his back. "I assume you already know what his report says."

Calls Thunder Song sighed. "If they intended to send help, there would be a party of magi coming this way now, ready to talk strategy and prepare. By sending one, the Council tells me what I need to know."

"Shit," Mangas breathed out, stirring the fire quietly with a worn hatchet.

Silence fell over the elders as they contemplated the fire. None of them could deny what they had experienced, first through the warnings of Calls Thunder Song beginning several seasons before, then finally through their own dreams and lodge trances. At first, just something off-center at the edge of their perceptions, then a shadow playing at the edge of eyesight. Turn to look, and it vanishes in the light. Eventually, even the least sensitive among them could feel it: a weight, oppressive and dank, a smothering darkness without direction. How Calls Thunder Song had stood it so long, none of the others knew. Now, after they had lived with the steadily increasing presence of it in the dreaming, even elders in friendly tribes were feeling it, though none were as capable, or close to Coyote, as Calls Thunder Song. Many thought the oldest and youngest of the tribe were sick more often and for longer since the presence invaded the dreaming, though none were sure.

"Well," Loup-Garou said, stretching his arms. The creak and pop of old joints was loud in the blistering lodge air. "We stand alone, Shoshone and one young magus. As usual, our chances are fantastic."

White Hawk snorted, arms folded across his broad chest. "And yet, here we sit, survivors of all the other times we stood alone against many fierce and deadly enemies. Have some faith, you cranky old goat."

Loup-Garou scowled, surprising no one. "Our enemies have always been flesh and blood warriors, fighting with knives and guns. Even the occasional shamans were only human. Whatever this is that Calls Thunder Song is sensing, that we all are sensing, is not."

"True," Calls Thunder Song said into the silence that followed Loup-Garou's words. "As Loup-Garou says, this blackness isn't human, and between that and the flood of whites from the east, our future is dim. We don't have many allies, my friends, but we do have them."

"This threat isn't just against us," Mangas said, his voice thoughtful. "The Bannock could have sensed it too, and the Paiute. A warning to them may be a good idea."

"Or it could be an excellent excuse for them to attack. How can we fight Bannock braves if we're scared of shadows?" Loup-Garou said to Mangas. "Should we borrow more trouble than we already have?"

"Trouble from enemies we know, human enemies? Better that than whatever this blackness holds," Mangas said, throwing the hatchet down by the fire.

"You have a point, but Loup-Garou is right," White Hawk said. "Bringing other tribes into this can only cause problems, not that they could help much anyway. What tribe has a shaman of Calls Thunder Song's ability? It grieves me to say this, but allies among the whites like this magus may be what we need to save our people."

The lodge fell silent at White Hawk's words. Every one of the men inside was an experienced warrior, and had a dim view at best of white men and their ways. Many Shoshone, Apache, Sioux and others, from too many tribes to count, had been the brunt of harsh dealings and worse from the whites. Seeking help from such "allies," even those from cordially neutral groups like the Council, was appalling. If any of the elders possessed any knowledge or experience of European religions, they might have called it heretical. But, Calls Thunder Song had sensed the blackness gathering at the edges of his perception for some time, and he didn't believe it would stop at the borders of Shoshone territory, nor Bannock or Paiute lands. It would swallow everything, until there was nothing more but itself.

"Let's put this aside for now," Calls Thunder Song told his fellow elders. "We can talk this over until Coyote steals the sun to no end. I suggest we bring the magus to us and find out what he knows."

"What could he--," Loup-Garou began.

"Enough," Calls Thunder Song said. The tone of his voice was short, hard. Shocked, Loup-Garou kept his peace. Many Voices kept his face stony only through an effort of will, but White Hawk was not as successful in keeping a smile from his face. The mighty elder warrior loved Loup-Garou like a brother, but that sometimes meant Loup-Garou annoyed him to no end.

"Fights the Wind is a capable shaman, but it will take him more than a day to reach us even with strong horses and his best spells," Calls Thunder Song told the elders. "It is time we met our newest guest by faster means. I will call on the dream walking to bring them here."

Almost as one, the elders nodded. Each of them expected this to happen, and so all were prepared. Quickly, the area around the fire was cleared to allow Calls Thunder Song space to make the traditional signs and dances. Many Voices brought forth a small drum of buffalo skin and tapped his fingers on the taut drumhead, listening to its thudding tone. From the depths of his ceremonial skins, Calls Thunder Song produced three small bags of herbs and weighed them in his hand. Loup-Garou handed the shaman a hunting spear, and White Hawk and Mangas helped him prepare his headdress and leggings for dream magic, hanging the correct feathers and beads while adjusting it on Calls Thunder Song's wiry, powerful frame.

Many Voices began the chanting, singing out a convoluted phrase in a clear, strong tenor voice. The other elders joined in, using the words of blessing and convocation as a foundation for the faster and more complex prayer line Calls Thunder Song would sing while dancing and placing the herbs. The shaman began his dance, calling on the spirits of world and sky to help summon the dream walking. At specific points in the dream circle, he shook Loup-Garou's hunting spear and scratched runes into the dirt with swift stabs.

An arc of crushed herbs flew from the shaman's hand into the fire, now leaping and roaring, flickering in time with the elders' chanting. Flames swirled and darted to catch the offering, and with a jet of lapis lazuli smoke and a flare of deep amber light, the lodge walls dissolved around them. No one faltered in the chanting, and Calls Thunder Song danced with renewed strength as the sky fell in furrowed sheets to join the earth in the shaman's spell. Stars blinked and wheeled, forming into a glittering bowled ceiling over the space of Calls Thunder Song's workings, which spread to enfold the entire visible universe within the few square feet of the waking world that was a Shoshone lodge. Walls faded into nothing as the air curdled and clotted around them.

It gets worse, a part of Calls Thunder Song's consciousness whispered as he recited the complex spell casting, continuing to scratch reinforcing runes into the earth as he did. *The darkness spreads even into the dream walking, curdling the word before it is spoken.*

Have a little faith, White Hawk's voice seemed to answer, and Calls Thunder Song smiled in his dancing. Another handful went into the fire, and the lodge space unfolded into the stars, then curved into another existence, finally settling in a valley where two men sat around a similar fire, talking over something in murmured voices. Outside the light of the campfire, nothing but mist and curdled air was visible. A lean, rangy man sat cross-legged before the flames, warming his pale hands, while a darker, more compact man leaned against a small shade tree, the clasp that held a bone knife in its sheath unfastened against the night.

As one, the chanting of the elders stopped on Calls Thunder Song's final syllable, and the shaman buried the tip of the hunting spear into the earth, pinning the two realities in place until the will to bind them was exhausted or the spirits tired of his efforts. Ripples, faint but visible, spread upward into the air from the spear, then faded as the lodge and campfire adjusted and became, temporarily, part of the same space. The dream walking was complete. All that remained was the first step.

Calls Thunder Song removed his headdress, placed the bags of herbs down at his place around the lodge fire, and stepped out of the lodge into his son's campsite, more than a hundred miles away. The magus from the Council, who was making an argument of some kind to Fights the Wind in rusty Shoshone, blinked repeatedly at the sight of the old shaman who'd suddenly walked out of thin air in front of him. While he'd expected this at some point—since the tribal encampment wouldn't be anywhere near a settler town on a railroad line— expecting it and actually seeing Calls Thunder Song perform a dream walking in the flesh were far different things for Aquinas. Teleportation was something beyond all but a few in the Council, and the actual joining of two physically disparate places separated by great distance was a sign of incredible power and, more importantly, control of that power to a fantastic degree.

"Hello, Aquinas Moore of the Western Council," Calls Thunder Song said in unaccented English. "I am Calls Thunder Song of the Shoshone, and we have a great problem before us."

Chapter 5

Damned loud echo in here, Lt. Caldwell thought as he strode toward Mr. Pineville's office, a thin sheaf of papers in his hand. Colonel Hamish McAlister had responded to Mr. Pineville's orders with typical Scotsman bluster, Caldwell thought, demanding a more precise set of objectives before taking his men much farther than they had gone. Although McAlister tactfully left out anything that could be viewed as insulting, Caldwell had heard the fiery officer curse cadets with verve and enthusiasm, and he suspected the telegraph officer's ears rang for a day after the colonel left. Furthermore, he was sure Pineville knew all the things McAlister didn't say, and didn't care. Pineville gave the impression of not being concerned by much except his railroad project.

The doors did not open at the lieutenant's approach; it was half past seven in the evening, and no one else was in the building. Caldwell half-expected Pineville to have gone home, but knew the odds were good the little brown suit of a man was still there. Maybe the cleaning staff just folds him up and stores him under that great bulk of a desk, Caldwell thought, like that automaton in the Hawthorne story. He grimaced at the unwelcome image of Pineville dancing wildly around his office, an unlucky partner in his arms.

Caldwell braced himself for a hard shove, but the doors opened easily at the slightest pressure of his hand. They made no noise as they swung open, revealing Mr. Pineville's office to be empty. The polished brass gas lamps were still lit, however, so Caldwell assumed Mr. Pineville simply stepped out for a moment and would soon return. The lieutenant mentally shrugged; there was no need to explain the correspondence, so he could leave it on Mr. Pineville's desk and head back to quarters, perhaps stop for dinner along the way.

As the lieutenant approached the massive desk, he noticed signs of Mr. Pineville's increasing occupation with the project. Usually, the official kept his work space sterile and neat, but now the desk was hardly visible under a blizzard of reports, requisitions, maps and a scattered sheaf of deeds, yellowed with age and spread among the other papers, a bureaucratic stratum of pages covering the hardwood surface. Only the immediate space around the desk lamp was clear, and that just barely. A pile of jumbled clothes and what looked like a blanket lay on the floor against the wall directly behind Mr. Pineville's chair, which seemed damned strange. Still, the lieutenant thought as he looked for a less-crowded space to leave the papers he brought, it's been so damn warm lately. Pineville might have brought a change of clothes so he didn't have to go home in a puddle.

Caldwell placed the papers on the bundle closest to the edge of the desk, figuring that would be where Pineville would look first. One of the papers on the side of the desk fluttered, disturbed by his passage, and slid to one side, revealing a map splashed with color and part of a heavily drawn geometric pattern on it. Caldwell knew immediately that he was looking at the proposed rail tracks, having worked with Pineville on that project for several months, but something about the pattern caught his eye. It was too regular, too machinelike to be what and where it was. He pushed a set of requisitions for hand equipment aside and picked up the map, holding it closer to the lamp's steady warm light.

Colors, a rich swirl of crimson and emerald, burst off the map under the light, almost wet in their dark glitter and covering the borders etched on the map in chromatic splendor. Several sheets of onion paper were fastened to the top of the map, and by carefully lifting the sheets, Caldwell saw several overlapping track plans were painstakingly traced on the delicate paper. He flipped the overlays over, curious as how the overall plan would look from a mapmaker's standpoint, but as more sheets revealed their singular patterns, the lieutenant's brow furrowed, and he felt a frown starting on his face.

Each sheet was dated with projected times of completion, along with actual dates if the line pictured was finished. Individually, the lines were nothing special, spurs and sidings and main lines between towns. Added up, a picture of something Caldwell felt he should recognize appeared. A series of arcs, curving around natural barriers and towns in some cases, interlocked near the middle of the pattern into a rough circle around a sizable piece of land, little of which was permanently settled. Around the circle, lines jutted off in numerous directions, heading off to larger junctions in Pocatello, Denver, Salt Lake City, Carson City and other rail towns throughout the West. Some of those lines, Caldwell saw, crossed into the rough circle made by the arcs. He held up the map against the lamp light and felt something cool cross the nape of his neck as recognition stole over him. The pattern within the circle was a pentagram, rough and misshapen but recognizable all the same.

"Must be a coincidence," Caldwell muttered, staring intently at the map as if to will away seeing the pattern. Using railroad tracks to build geometric shapes on the land only God could recognize didn't make any sense, especially in a shape that was used in ancient rituals. What possible reason could there be for Pineville—for it had to be Pineville's doing; he was responsible for directing the various construction efforts—to have a miles-long symbol built out of rails and beams? Wood and iron didn't make…

A mostly-forgotten piece of lore shambled out of his memory, something he'd read in the fairy tales and fantasies of his youth. Something about cold iron, he thought. What did that have to do with anything? Looking at the map, Caldwell wondered if this could be definitive proof Mr. Pineville had taken leave of his senses. The man must need a long rest, to come up with such a plan and devote hundreds of men and thousands upon thousands of dollars to making it happen, he thought with a rising sense of disappointment. Caldwell wondered if he should report this, and if so, how much would have to be redone in surveying, even if it turned out that some or most of the proposed lines could be saved. The scope of the scandal would be devastating, once the public got wind of how much was spent.

Lost in thought, wondering how much of the work could be saved, Caldwell didn't hear the rustling behind him at first. The sound, low and slithery, sounded like the hiss of gas jets. *This will have to be reported*, the lieutenant thought as he calculated a rough estimate of the cost to date. *Mr. Pineville had better have a good explanation for this.*

"As a matter of fact, there is an explanation," a low, garbled voice said behind him.

The lieutenant turned around, a greeting already half-spoken when he registered what had been speaking. Words died on his lips as he watched Pineville return. Caldwell had seen the clothes on the floor, and what he thought was a blanket, but hadn't looked closely. Now, as a hunched and twisted shape gained weight and straightened one miserable inch at a time, he realized that the pale garment he mistook for a blanket was actually skin. Mr. Pineville's skin, which was returning to human proportions as the shape slowly inflated, like a hot air balloon with a fire beneath. Even as it gained definition, sheets of flesh becoming arms and legs, masses turning into hands and head, the thing that dressed in Mr. Pineville spoke.

"Lieutenant, you are a rare individual in Washington these days. Hard-working, intelligent, and possessed of a rather strong imagination for a young officer."

The thing paused, took a step as if to regain its balance. It had almost regained Mr. Pineville's full dimensions; now it simply looked as though Mr. Pineville was made of wax and brought too close to a flame. Sagging features ran and folded into their proper shapes, and the glitter of oily pools in the thing's eye sockets slowly returned to a more human shade of Pineville's usual brown. The transformation was horrifying, making Caldwell's heart stutter in his chest, but somehow fascinating to watch. Caldwell was not particularly religious or superstitious, but here was proof positive that something more than human experience was in the world, and under the terror, Caldwell felt the beginnings of something he hadn't felt in years: wonder.

Whatever wore Mr. Pineville's skin managed to firm up its face, opening its mouth wide several times to work the jaw and teeth into their proper place. It spoke again. "It would be rather a waste to kill you now, Lieutenant, after all the work you've put in."

Caldwell said nothing, watching the last pieces of the change fall into place as wrinkles vanished and bones popped back into sockets with audible snaps and crunches. The process was fascinating, but vile and against every natural law and precept he ever studied or observed. Somewhere in his heart, he knew what he had seen could not be benign; such a horrifying thing must have poisonous intentions against his country, even possibly the world. And yet…he had never seen such power, such *intent.* What could appear out of nowhere and wear a man like a suit? What possible purpose could such a thing have?

The lieutenant looked at the thing that wore Mr. Pineville, and the thing looked back, an amused smile crossing its face. Each knew what Caldwell was thinking: he had to know. Evil, good, incomprehensible to man, Caldwell had to know.

"You'll do for now, Lieutenant," the thing that wore Mr. Pineville's skin said, and grinned from ear to ear, stretching wide to expose hardened gums and yellowed teeth in a smile that was jovial, open and as far as Caldwell could see, completely empty of humanity.

Even as part of Lieutenant Caldwell's mind screamed in horror, he said, "Thank you, Mr. Pineville."

Chapter 6

"You didn't know anything of this?" Fights the Wind said, nostrils flaring but otherwise calm. He sat to the right of his father, across the lodge fire from Aquinas. The magus was breathing regularly, forcing himself to quell his nerves at being seated between White Hawk and Loup-Garou, neither one of them happy sitting so close to a white man. Mangas sat to the left of Loup-Garou, seemingly unconcerned with the arrangement, while Many Voices sat outside the reach of the fire's light.

Aquinas shook his head. "On the Council's orders, the packet was sealed with a geas. Only Calls Thunder Song or another Council member could open it, and I was ordered not to, in very clear terms." *Standard procedure for diplomatic packets*, Aquinas thought, *and you know this. What did you find so upsetting?*

Calls Thunder Song nodded. "As would be expected; the Council's practice hasn't changed in centuries." The old shaman sighed, exhausted from the dream walking and reading the Council's mind-numbing diplomatic language. "Mangas, find Mr. Moore a place to sleep for the night; he's our guest until further notice."

"Mr. Moore, we must speak," Calls Thunder Song said as Mangas got to his feet and left the lodge. "Some of this concerns you very much, and we must come to agreement."

White Hawk snorted and followed Mangas out of the lodge, grumbling. With a silent nod toward the shaman, Many Voices and Loup-Garou took their leave. Fights the Wind glared into the darkness behind Aquinas.

"The Council is aware of the blackness I've sensed," Calls Thunder Song began, "although they cannot feel it as strongly as we do. They don't know what to call it, but there is some consensus of what it might be."

Aquinas nodded. "How can I help?"

The ancient shaman smiled brightly, looking uncannily like his son in the shimmering light. "You'll have time to ponder that, Mr. Moore. The Council is pleased to inform you that you've been assigned as a diplomatic liaison to my people for now." He handed a sheet of paper over to the stunned magus. "Congratulations on your promotion."

Carefully—irritating a shaman of Calls Thunder Song's caliber seemed like a poor idea, even if mildly—Aquinas took the paper from the shaman's hand and pored over the brief paragraphs. It was a formal notice of diplomatic posting, assigning one Aquinas L. Moore to act as the special diplomatic liaison to the Western Aboriginal Confederacy, a blanket term the Council often used when referring to the assorted tribes of the West. A secondary set of instructions at the bottom laid out his classification, pay grade (*how nice, a salary*, his inner voice chuckled) and specific instructions stating he would be stationed with the Shoshone under Calls Thunder Song for the duration of his assignment.

"I don't understand," Aquinas said. "Is there a treaty being discussed?"

"I'll never understand how government officials think," Calls Thunder Song said casually to his son, who finally looked away from the darkness to meet his father's gaze. "The white settlers out here may regret the government that came with them one day."

"Sir, the Council isn't the same as the government," Aquinas said.

Both shamans turned to look at Aquinas with identical expressions, and he realized how foolish he sounded. "I apologize. What I mean is, the Council has different goals in mind than the federal government. I don't know what the Council intended, but since they didn't give me any specific details about this assignment, or in fact tell me about it at all, I presume they want me to act on my own best judgment."

Fights the Wind laughed out loud, a grin creasing his features as chuckles boomed off the lodge's rough walls and ceiling. "New to government work, aren't you?"

"Mr. Moore, what my son means is that you weren't given details because there are none to give," Calls Thunder Song said. "The Council knows there's something here, but they don't know what, and since they know less than I do, they're unwilling to commit anything more than a token gesture."

"Only the fact my father is known and respected throughout the world motivated the Council to send anyone at all," Fights the Wind said, his eyes unreadable once again. "Until something more is known about this threat, you'll be staying with us, Mr. Moore, and doing whatever you can."

"This brings me back to my question, sir," Aquinas said to Calls Thunder Song. "How can I help? What is this blackness you're sensing? Possession? Vengeful spirits? One of the Fey Folk attacking humans? I cannot help you without some idea of what you're facing."

"There have been no attacks, yet," Fights the Wind replied. "No sightings, no signs or omens. My father has sensed some presence in the dream walking, something that inhibits casting."

"It has progressed for some time," Calls Thunder Song said, his eyes thoughtful. "I first sensed it some years ago, but just barely. I thought at first it was something bleeding over from a curse of some kind; many have been cast recently, mostly against the Army, and it's difficult not to find some traces of that in the dreaming."

"At first?"

The ancient shaman nodded. "Over time, I realized it couldn't be a curse, or even curses. The darkness was too consistent, too singular. It's vague and shapeless, but it has a meaning, a destiny behind it. And it's growing stronger." Calls Thunder Song hesitated and reached up to touch the sacred medicine bag he wore around his neck, a gesture that sent a trickle of fear racing up Aquinas' spine. For something to frighten a shaman who made wagers with gods...

"I've felt something similar once before," Calls Thunder Song continued. "Something equally dark and ominous, though not with the same sense of purpose or vastness behind it."

Fights the Wind's eyes opened wide. "You never mentioned this, father."

"It was only recently I recognized the touch, and even now I'm not sure what I sensed. I only have the dream sensing to guide me so far, and even that's like capturing smoke." Calls Thunder Song sighed, a long exhalation that seemed to leave him smaller as the breath escaped. "I pray I'm wrong."

The cold sense of fear that started as a trickle was now an icy river down Aquinas' back, a river of hypothermia that stole the air from his lungs. Many kinds of dark magic existed, almost as many as there were deities, spirits and loas to which it could be invoked, but only a few could represent such a threat to a shaman, and none of those were anything Aquinas ever dealt with before.

"What do you think it is?" Aquinas asked.

Calls Thunder Song sighed again, and said a word long

and thorny in a dialect that Aquinas did not recognize. He frowned and looked at Fights the Wind, who turned pale at his father's answer. The younger shaman looked at his father and asked a question in the same dialect. Calls Thunder Song nodded and spoke for several seconds, the words flowing and twisting almost visibly in the air. Even as Aquinas waited for Fights the Wind to translate, he marveled at the fluidity and power of the language in which the shaman spoke. *If I were a logomancer, I would dream of being able to use such a dialect in my spells*, Aquinas thought, and wondered if he would have been better off had he chosen the reclusive researcher path to magic.

Too late, his subconscious chortled in Uncle Simon's voice, not without sympathy.

Fights the Wind looked at Aquinas, his gaze troubled. "My father is not entirely sure, but he believes the darkness to be a sign of a renegade practice, supposed to be extinct. I don't know the word in English, but it requires the purposeful killing of people."

Aquinas' heart seemed to freeze solid. "Sacrifices?"

Fights the Wind shook his head. "Not to call something from other worlds or to appease a being. This uses the crossing over to generate power for the casting; energy released from human death propels the spell into being. My father says for large spells, it takes the killing of several people all at once."

The world around Aquinas slowed as the blood rushed through his body, a spike of fear tingling his skin as a word, dredged from the depths of his memory, leaped to his lips. "Necromancy."

Calls Thunder Song nodded. "I don't know the word, but I can tell from your face it's the right one. You know of this."

Aquinas looked from one shaman to another. His tongue

felt slablike and swollen as he tried to speak. The air of the lodge was very close, as if several men were huddled under a buffalo hide, and the magus fought the urge to run from the warming fire, find the nearest horse, and ride as far and as fast as it could take him. "We need to speak to the Council."

"What would we say? I have no proof," Calls Thunder Song said, shaking his head. "My reputation isn't enough to force the Council to take action, and they won't want to believe this. I don't want to believe this, Mr. Moore, and yet I sense it."

The shaman stood up slowly, his hand on his son's shoulder. Aquinas saw the subtle tension of muscles and knew Fights the Wind was supporting his father's weight. "We cannot fight something we cannot identify. In the morning, we'll discuss how to determine if what I sense is truly this...necromancy. For now, we must rest. Come, step out of the lodge so we can release the dream walking, unless you'd like a long walk tomorrow."

Aquinas and Fights the Wind nodded their agreement and followed the ancient shaman out the door.

Chapter 7

Moonlight glimmered like water off the twin iron rails, lighting a path beside the station and into the darkness beyond the depot, where no lights burned. The porter, sitting on a caboose's boarding platform, amused himself some nights by staring into the void and looking ahead at what would be wrought in those great lands in the likely future to come. Some things he saw were monstrous, frightening even to immortals and gods, but the porter saw the hope of enough laughter to keep his mood light, although he was deeply saddened at the thought of railroads fading into insignificance. Traveling by train, the porter thought, might have been one of the humans' better developments, along with coffee and the written word.

Footsteps sounded in the loose gravel by the tracks. The porter finished his cigarette, extinguished the burning ember with a wink, and flicked the butt into the night away from the depot. *Maybe some lizard will develop a taste for tobacco and create religion*, the porter thought, grinning at the thought. He grabbed the handrail and hopped to his feet, ready to help his visitor to the platform.

The footsteps stopped short of where the light was, keeping his visitor's face shaded. Not that he didn't know who it was, but the porter had known her for a long time, and she did like a little air of mystery now and then. It had served their first marriage well enough, he supposed.

"Why black?" her voice rang out, strong and smooth in the moony air.

A great grin crossed his features as he looked down, appearing perfectly mortal in his uniform, creased and still sharp, buttons and insignia bright as the contrasting night could make them. "It goes with the uniform. Not a lot of our people working on railroads yet, unless you count the occasional bandit or laborer."

"No," the visitor said, accepting the porter's offer of a hand up. Even standing on the caboose's shaded platform, half-lit by the moon, she was striking. Piercing black eyes, a face with the sharp and terrible beauty of a saber, and a strong and curved body that men—white, black, red and any other human shade that could be found—would fight tooth and nail to tumble with under starlight or between sheets. The porter loved her still, and if she ever forgave him for a midnight dalliance with a water spirit—or three, he'd lost track—he would love her again and again, as much as he could give.

"Nice to see you again," the porter said. "Care to give me a hand with this little project the white men have going on around here?"

"What, the railroads?" the visitor said. "You know how that's going to end up. Binding the land with iron and smoke was inevitable. Still seems foolish to me, but it's working well enough."

"You know better, Eagle Woman. Been in the dreaming lately? It's all over the place, between the basic vibrations and one of our children looking for it. I'm surprised all the Spirit Councils aren't out searching."

Eagle Woman snorted, an indelicate noise that was oddly fetching coming from her. The porter decided he'd beg her forgiveness again and see if it got him anywhere. That water spirit was centuries ago anyway.

"Perhaps if you hadn't decided to get a mortal job, you'd

be a little better informed, dear former husband. The Spirit Councils are on the hunt, all of them, calling in old favors and summoning the antiquities from their resting places. Every manitowak for 500 miles is on the loose. Even Kaknu is up and around, sniffing out whatever the old bastard can find."

The porter's eyebrows rose in the darkness, a gesture wasted on Eagle Woman, still looking out into the empty night as if searching for Spirit Council hunters. "Well, serving food and drink on the railroad isn't like hunting vague threats, but it has its pleasures. And uses, too. It's not only our people on the hunt, now."

Eagle Woman laughed, a dark bitter echo of the music the porter remembered. "The whites don't care what happens. Unless this…whatever it is comes dressed in a crucifix and martyr's clothes, they'll ignore it until everything goes away."

The porter laughed uneasily; none of the Spirit Councils liked the whites, but they had a place in destiny too, and dismissing them out of hand did not sit well with the porter. "They've sent a magus to help."

"A whole magus? I'll tell the Spirit Councils and we can all retire," Eagle Woman replied.

The porter shook his head and idly cast a bit of magic with a flick of his fingers; a harmless prank, just to see if his magic could slip past her defenses. He saw nothing—the magic of gods is often too subtle to see, even to their eyes—but he felt the arc bounce and skitter as his prank was turned aside, deflecting harmlessly into the high desert soil. Rocks and dust flew in a small geyser, and he was certain he heard something small and many-legged scuttle away at high speed. *Damn*, he thought, *she's still got it.*

"The point is there's some effort there, even if a small one. One magus isn't enough, but it's one more resource than they had before. You really have become bitter, former wife. Lighten up."

"And what will you do?" she asked the porter.

The porter shrugged. "What can I do? I'm just a humble porter, serving biscuits and coffee on the Santa Fe-Denver-Portland line."

"I'll tell Coyote the next time he asks for you. What name shall I give him when he wants to talk?"

Again, the great grin spread across the porter's face. "Just tell him Trickster, for now. Some ham-headed Norse jerk already has Loki locked down."

Eagle Woman smiled back, but her face, lean and flawless, did not look amused. "That's a bold move, husband. Coyote might not appreciate the game."

"He appreciates nothing but the game, wife. Besides, even if he decides to make a move, the stain on the dreaming remains. What news do the Spirit Councils bring, as if I didn't know?"

The porter's former wife sighed, losing some of her fearsome aspect in the process. Now, she looked almost human, even in the dim light from the sky. *What in Creation was I thinking*, the porter wondered for a second. A memory intruded then, of a lithesome water spirit and how she moved against him in the rushes and weeds of a starless night. *Ah*, the porter thought, *that's right*.

"Unfocused. Broad. Menacing, but to who or what, nobody seems to know. It's a general impression more than anything, but that strong…it has to be someone very skilled, or very angry, or something so big even its newborn steps shake the dreaming."

"Or something very new and unknown to us," the porter mused. A wisp of idea came to him, and he chased it down the paths and furrows of his thoughts, unaware of the silence hovering over the two immortal beings standing on a rough-hewn caboose platform. Like smoke, however, the thought eluded him, and he came back to his consciousness to find his former wife staring at him. Her eyes were wide and...well, if Eagle Woman were human, he might have thought fearful. But she was not, so he did not. Such thoughts were dangerous if Eagle Woman sensed them; she wasn't amused by such perceptions, the porter knew, and she could be...vengeful.

"That's a disturbing suggestion," Eagle Woman finally said.

The porter nodded, agreeing with her completely. Tricksters were mischievous and inventive by nature, but occasionally, unpleasant ideas came to their minds, and the porter was afraid of what he'd thought. In his lengthy experience, the most unpleasant ideas sprang into being with the greatest regularity. He knew of nearly all the mystical, magical and otherworldly creatures and beings that resided in what humans thought of as the world, and the idea there might be one he didn't know opened up a host of possibilities, few of them good.

"I fear it's an idea we must share with the Spirit Councils," the porter said heavily. The thought of standing before the Spirit Councils again, only a few brief centuries after his last head-to-head with Coyote and the resultant not-so-forcible exile, filled him with a sluggish sense of distaste and dread, but there wasn't going to be much choice in the matter. It was his idea, after all, and that meant it was his responsibility to carry it to his people. Besides, he would never drop such a burden on Eagle Woman, even if he was still a little bit angry at her throwing him out.

"I fear you're right," Eagle Woman said, "and we best do it quickly. Coyote will want to know of this."

"We've another stop to make first," the porter said; his mental will o' the wisp had returned, and it brought a friend. This time, however, he let the idea come to him, and it rewarded him by providing another fleeting scrap of information. "We should share this with our mortal children. They're in the thick of this whatever, and they'll be in the best spot to use anything we can pass on."

"Coyote will speak with Calls Thunder Song after you speak to the Spirit Councils."

"It's not Calls Thunder Song I had in mind," the porter said, remembering a brilliant braided aura on a Pullman car just a sliver of human time before. With that, the decision was made. The porter jumped down onto the loose dirt and gravel by the tracks and held out his hand purely by reflex. Eagle Woman eyed his hand as if he'd offered her a used handkerchief. *Amazing*, the porter thought, *how quickly habits form amongst the mortals. I've only been doing this job for a decade.*

Eagle Woman nodded, her expression unreadable as she gazed at the porter's outstretched hand. The porter almost dropped his reach, but she finally took it as she stepped gracefully from the platform, her long fingers folding gently around his. Her skin was warm, firm as leather but yielding, and a charge of electric potential seemed to leap into his skin from hers, making his hand and wrist tingle. Neither dropped their clasp.

"I continue to beg—," the porter began.

"Later," Eagle Woman said softly. "If there is time, we can discuss this and all else later."

Silence fell between them, soft and fragile in the jagged starlit night. The porter held her hand for a moment longer, then reluctantly opened his fingers. Eagle Woman withdrew her hand, sliding her fingertips lightly over his roughened palm.

"Fair enough," the porter said gently. "Let's go speak

with a magus."

Turning, they walked into the obsidian nightfall beyond the parked caboose and its wan lantern light, guided only by the shimmering of ley lines and their preternatural perceptions. Five steps, then six, and a part of the world folded around them as they passed into the dreaming, as natural a state to them as sunlight. An observer who could see such workings might have noticed a denting in the fabric of reality as they walked forward, then the gentle give as the dreaming accepted them, and the smooth flowing as reality regained its natural shape, no worse the wear for its temporary transformation.

The hardpan beneath his borrowed bedroll (he had been too tired even to summon his own, a simple unfolding requiring virtually no energy to start) was unyielding, but Aquinas knew that wasn't what kept him tossing. Physically, he was exhausted, the welling of energy from a nearby land meridian the only thing keeping him from fatigue paralysis. Mentally, he was a long way from sleep.

If Calls Thunder Song was correct—and there was no reason to think he wasn't; the shaman's sensitivity and skill were legend—then horrors were not far behind. Demonic possession was almost preferable. At least a demon could be cast out into incorporeal form and sent packing, or even killed with the proper equipment and personnel. Necromancy was outlawed for many reasons, not the least of which—besides the obvious moral sinkhole of an art that depended on murder, and immense amounts of it—was that death magic is both hideously potent and virtually impossible to control. Even a simple necromantic spell could generate unforeseeable side effects: violent and repulsive behavior of mortals for a hundred miles in every direction, spontaneous generation of monsters from human and animal stock, mysterious substances with unusual and lethal effect, all of which and more had been reported after necromantic activity.

According to some ancient journals, accessible to only the most senior Council members and thus the subject of many rumors, necromantic spells had, on thankfully rare occasion, opened doors to worlds unknown by man or demon, places where even the fundamental physical laws were hostile to life. Aquinas heard such things during his schooling; even as a young man convinced of his immortality, he'd found the rumors alone to be disturbing, and all those inchoate fears rushed back to nestle in his racing mind.

And what can you do about it now, his subconscious devil's advocate asked. *Whether it is necromancy or not, you can do nothing if you are exhausted. Put these thoughts away for now and return to them tomorrow.*

Easier said than done, Aquinas knew, but conceded the point. He leadenly turned onto his left side, facing the nearest wall of the empty lodge. Too tired to be concerned with his exposed back, Aquinas closed his eyes and practiced breathing exercises to drain his wakefulness away. Slowly, a sensation of release and cooling muscle tension seeped its way up his limbs, and Aquinas began to hope sleep would take him before the sun rose. The wind scampered around the guest lodge, as if to lull him to sleep with its low whistling tune.

Nearly asleep, Aquinas felt in his being a minute change in tension in the world, so subtle at first he thought he'd slipped into the private dreaming no one else can share. A lightening of the air on his skin, bringing a slight touch of coolness, brought him awake, while simultaneously the humidity changed to a crisper, more arid feel. A strong, swampy smell of a nearby marsh struck him, as did the scent of lilies and, somewhat strangely, jasmine. His ears could no longer hear cinders pop and smolder in the fire pit; instead, moving water and the chattering of cicadas filled the night. Beneath his bedroll, the rough ground seemed easier to settle into, more willing to comfort.

"Comfortable, magus?" a voice said behind him.

In the depths of his mind, Aquinas ordered his body to turn quickly and prepare for a fight, but he was too weighted with exhaustion, and it seemed to take hours before he managed to turn. The voice's timbre had been male and somewhat familiar. After forcing himself to move away from sleep, the magus rolled onto his back and looked into the porter's face, no more than a foot away and grinning as widely as the magus had ever seen a human face manage.

Aquinas mumbled something with a sleep-thickened tongue. The porter laughed gleefully, which didn't help Aquinas rouse himself at all.

"I'm not familiar with that dialect," the porter said. "I thought I knew most human languages."

The magus swallowed hard and tried again. "What are you, and what do you want?"

"Admirably to the point," Eagle Woman said, stepping through the soft place in reality's folds. Her face was closer to human now, the hard edges of her high cheekbones and bladed nose fading to more common proportions, but her pitiless eyes were still otherworldly. Aquinas, slowly waking up to his situation, was unsure of which being to fear more in the long run. The porter had an inhuman aura, and Aquinas didn't need to check if the woman's was as well. Sharp tangs of ozone and thundercloud filled his nostrils.

Eagle Woman gracefully sat by the porter in one smooth motion, facing Aquinas patiently as he raced to grasp his situation. His eyes met hers, and the magus was filled with an instant sense of transparency, as if the eldritch beauty saw through his bones and skin and muscle to examine the intricate workings of his magic and soul. It was an oddly intimate sensation, and not unpleasant.

"Aquinas," the woman said, shaping each syllable with precise diction. A tinge of accent, something deeper than any human tongue, caressed her words. "An unusual name for a magus."

"Eagle Woman," the porter said, his voice flat. "Let's talk to the magus, not quiz him on family histories." The porter, who Aquinas—now fully awake—recognized from his train ride, smiled again, showing just a bright sliver of teeth. The magus felt his heart accelerate like a train engine in his chest.

"As you wish," Eagle Woman said. She turned to face Aquinas more fully, subtly shutting the porter out of her line of sight. The sense of an age-old game, crosses and moves and rules incomprehensible, stole over Aquinas, and he resolved to tread carefully. Magical beings tended to value games far more than the mortals sometimes trapped in them.

"What do you know about the darkness in the dreaming?" she asked the magus.

Aquinas shook his head. "Only what Calls Thunder Song has told me. It's strong, pervasive and more ominous than anything he's sensed before." He hesitated briefly. "He believes it may be caused by necromancy."

The porter's smile vanished. "Did he say why?"

"Just that he felt something similar before. The last recorded instance of necromancy that the Council knows of was over a century ago, and other than the immediate destruction, very little is known about it. Maybe this is what Calls Thunder Song meant."

The porter turned his head to face Eagle Woman. Her

gaze met his, and they appeared to have a conversation in looks and blinks. Aquinas watched them and wondered briefly at their history. Eagle Woman was a powerful figure in aboriginal American mythology, a god to some tribes, hardly more than an animal totem in others; to Aquinas, the reality tilted favorably toward god. Who the porter was, Aquinas had no idea. Still, to be so close to Eagle Woman, he must be powerful, Aquinas decided.

After a minute or more of silence, the porter looked away from Eagle Woman and faced Aquinas again. "We don't know what is causing this coming darkness, but whatever it is, it isn't necromancy, not at its root."

"There is necromantic casting underway," Eagle Woman said, "but it is not a necromancer performing the spellweaving, and no death energy has been generated yet."

Aquinas felt his jaw drop. "How can that be? Necromantic spells have to be cast very close to the energy generation; the potency falls off too fast."

"You are an expert necromancer?" the porter asked, a trace of his smile returning. Aquinas flushed at the jibe.

"No, but that much is known to the Council. Only a necromancer can cast such a spell."

"It isn't a necromancer," Eagle Woman said, her eyes flashing. "The signature, the aura is too different: whatever entity is weaving the spell is patient, very powerful and not human in any degree. And, as we've said, no death energy has been generated. Yet."

"Whatever it plans, it must be immense," Aquinas said, "if Calls Thunder Song and you can already sense it."

"I understand why Calls Thunder Song thought it might be a curse; it has some of that same texture to it, the same malevolence," the porter mused.

"He mentioned--," Aquinas began, but stopped as a thought struck him cold. What made the shaman think it was a curse? Still fogged from exhaustion, Aquinas wrestled with his memory. Calls Thunder Song said he felt it was a curse because...he expected a curse. That kind of magic was easily felt in the dreaming, likely due to the exquisite emotional sensitivity most humans felt in the dreaming, which was one major reason why shamans traveled in it as often as possible and cast their best spells there. But to feel a curse so strongly, one had to experience many of them...

... many have been cast recently, mostly against the Army...

"Oh, hell," Aquinas breathed softly as an idea, bright and terrible as a stake burning, resolved itself in his mind. "My God, that's..."

"You know what this is?" the porter asked.

"No," Aquinas said, "but I think I might know what part of the caster's plan is." The idea refused to fade, demanding his attention, but he knew if he were to fully regard it, he would become physically ill. Or worse; if it was true, and the U.S. military was being used as part of a plan to cast an immense spell, whoever or whatever was behind the plan was far stronger than he feared. A plan such as this, even in part, required a great deal of analysis and ability.

"Please excuse me for a moment," Aquinas said, stomach clenching with fear.

"For what?" Eagle Woman said sharply.

The magus looked at the two preternatural beings in his lodge. Finally, he had become fully awake, and now, dearly wished he hadn't.

"I think I need to pray," Aquinas said.

Chapter 8

Clouds of coal smoke puffed from the locomotive, signaling travel in its near future. Lt. Caldwell, for what seemed like the thousandth time since he woke at five that morning, wished travel wasn't in his, considering his traveling companion for the next six days.

"Lieutenant Caldwell," a voice behind him said. "Shall we board?"

Mr. Pineville was standing on the platform, a valise at his side and two tickets in his left hand. He was dressed as usual (in someone's skin, the lieutenant thought), clean and well-pressed in office clerk brown. Other travelers took notice of the lieutenant, dressed sharply in his uniform blues and polished boots, but their eyes slid right off Mr. Pineville. He wondered if anyone else actually saw the mousy exterior, or if they were avoiding him because, on some level, they sensed the thing inside the suit.

"Good morning, sir," Caldwell said. It took an effort, but his voice stayed clear and level.

Pineville acknowledged the greeting, gestured toward the train. Since the night Pineville's true nature was revealed, Caldwell sensed a number of changes in the official. He spoke more openly about the particulars of his tactics, although he kept tight-lipped on the overall strategy. More to the point, he treated Caldwell with a little more warmth and good humor, a situation that made the lieutenant deeply nervous.

"I've rented us a Pullman," Pineville said as they climbed

onboard. "We can discuss business there in peace."

The nape of Caldwell's neck tensed, but he nodded. He was undoubtedly afraid of Pineville, no question, but on those rare moments the lieutenant was able to think about his situation calmly, he admitted he was fascinated as well. What in the hell was he? Obviously not human, but what did that leave? What was his plan? Caldwell knew the answer to none of these questions, but he wanted to know, and he suspected that curiosity allowed him to continue living. At some level, it seemed to amuse Pineville, and that amusement value prevented Caldwell's life from ending, because the lieutenant suffered no doubt Pineville could kill him at any time. Any creature capable of wearing a human suit was likely capable of creating the suit in the first place, regardless of the original owner's opinion.

"Westward ho," Pineville said, smiling as they walked through the cabin, passing through the press of passengers and luggage. Sometimes, watching the cities slowly empty as people packed up and headed to the open states and empty places of the West, Caldwell thought God was slowly tilting His country up and tumbling the loose people out of all the settled places in the East and South, leaving only the rooted and contented behind. Caldwell tipped his hat to a well-dressed matron in a wine-dark dress, and wished he were heading west as part of this tumbling movement, for the same reasons and with a better companion than he had.

Pineville stopped before a sliding door with a darkly tinted window set inside it and opened it slowly as Caldwell reached the entryway. The official nodded at the interior as if greeting someone and stepped inside. As the lieutenant followed, he pulled up short as a uniformed colonel stood to shake hands with Pineville. The lieutenant saluted, belatedly recognizing Colonel McAlister of the Tenth Cavalry. McAlister smartly returned the salute.

"Lieutenant Caldwell," the colonel said. His gruff voice carried into the hallway, roughened from years of training soldiers and sending them into battle. McAlister's storied career in the Union forces led to an appointment at West Point, where he taught for many years, up until Caldwell's second year at the academy. Rumor had it discipline at West Point was not as stringent as McAlister liked, so he'd put in for a transfer into the field, defending towns and settlements in the western territories from Indian attack. Whatever the reason, McAlister lost no time in getting back into battle, and now here he was, face to face with Pineville. The crawling sensation on the nape of Caldwell's neck returned.

"Sir," Caldwell replied, words failing him. McAlister turned to Pineville, dismissing the lieutenant, and Caldwell found himself strangely relieved. The colonel's attention was no better or worse than any other ranking officer's, but with Pineville around, the lieutenant discovered his unease only deepened.

"Mr. Pineville, I believe I underestimated you. After our last discussion, I was surprised to find orders in my latest dispatch directing me to meet with you. I wasn't aware you had such pull with the general staff." McAlister's face and voice were even, but Caldwell saw the subtle twitch of muscle in the colonel's granite jaw and the banked fire in his gaze, heard the precise pronunciation and pitch of each word.

"I wouldn't call it pull, Colonel. The general staff were simply convinced by my arguments that we needed to have a direct discussion with you. You understand some things are better not discussed by telegraph." The expression on Pineville's face wasn't quite a smile, but the tone was there.

Caldwell wondered if McAlister, mere inches from a towering rage, would strike Pineville, feel the slide of skin over something other than muscle and bone, and realize something was wrong. A fist squeezed the lungs in the lieutenant's chest, driving the air from him in a silent exhale.

McAlister snorted. "Espionage? Unless you have a secret fort in the middle of nowhere, there's nothing to be hidden about this railroad project. You've wasted my time, Mr. Pineville."

Pineville laughed. "Not at all, Colonel. There are certain details that need to be ironed out, certain objectives we need to clarify. Most importantly, it's time for you to meet some of the higher-ups behind this project. The central planner, in particular, would like to meet you."

The fist in Caldwell's chest squeezed harder, touching his heart with icy fingers while his breath whistled in his ears. Beyond the big window in the car, the sun continued its cheerful morning duties, spreading sunlight like honey over the land, but seeming to stop at the glass pane. He opened his mouth to object, to shout a warning to the colonel, and a feeling like a bony claw dipped in velvet grabbed his head, enveloping his face and jaw in its unmoving grasp. Against his will, he felt the muscles of his lips and jaws relax, closing his mouth and placing an attentive expression on his face. Pineville, the lieutenant saw, appeared not to notice.

McAlister frowned, not noticing the lieutenant's silent struggle. "This is a government project; why would the secretary—," he started.

Pineville held up a hand. "The government was, like your superior officers, convinced to take this particular project through the efforts of…well, an outside consultant. It is this consultant who wants to meet you, discuss your future work on the project and your skills that make you invaluable."

"This is damned irregular," McAlister said.

"I understand," Pineville said, "but after you meet with the consultant, I think you will see the value in the project and the unorthodox way in which we have implemented it. Please, come with me, Colonel. The consultant has taken another car; we can go and have the meeting right now."

Caldwell's vision was starting to dim at the edges, the air in his chest congealed and devoid of life while the grip on his heart and head showed no weakness. Pineville's control of his body, he realized, was nearly absolute and virtually effortless on his part. Every struggle for movement, for air and voice barely manifested as a shifting of his weight; the lieutenant understood, in a flash of despairing insight, it was within Pineville's ability to strangle him to death with McAlister looking on, none the wiser as his body died and stood empty like a marionette in a trunk. *Or a suit hanging in a closet*, a voice whispered in his mind, eerily like Pineville's.

Your fate is to watch, the voice continued, and Caldwell knew it was no simulacrum in his mind. It was Pineville speaking to him, and he could have no secrets ever again Pineville couldn't take. Wild laughter echoed in his ears.

"Lieutenant, please complete the preliminary draftings before the colonel and I return," Mr. Pineville said, standing to leave. McAlister looked less enthusiastic, but stood as well. Caldwell nodded his head against his will and snapped a salute to the colonel, which was again smartly returned. A trickle of air seeped into his lungs as his body walked down the corridor toward a goal he did not know, followed by the last words he knew he would ever hear McAlister say. "Very well, Pineville. What's this consultant's name?"

"His name is quite long and difficult to pronounce, but he

likes being called the First," Pineville said.

The slamming of the compartment door behind him cut off the rest of Pineville's conversation with McAlister, and Caldwell's feet continued to march him through the rail car. Again the fist in Caldwell's chest squeezed, and he suddenly understood he had been completely wrong all along about his value to Pineville, that the official—or whatever it was that wore the official's once-human visage—only kept him around until it had someone of more immediate use to his ends, someone of more influence and position. *Much like Colonel McAlister*, the last gasp of Caldwell's rational mind said. *Exactly like him, in fact.*

Would you like to know His full name, lieutenant, the name that cannot yet be spoken in this realm? Pineville's voice said, teasing, almost playful in the core of his deepest thoughts. *Since nobody else can hear me in here, there's no reason you can't hear it. Keep a positive outlook, Lieutenant; it's entirely possible the damage caused to you will be minimal.*

Pineville laughed, and the whispering began. Below the alien syllables of rhythms and sounds no human palate could make, Caldwell felt the thrumming of a Power, the still-weak but terrible focus of an attention far beyond any nightmare he'd ever known.

Look upon this sliver, this fraction of awareness that bears the unspeakable name, Pineville's voice continued, *and be humbled.* A vision opened in Caldwell's head, monstrous in size and incandescent brilliance. Something turned Its eye to the lieutenant, now completely blind to the physical world, and Caldwell saw an endless abyss open before him, edged by fire and the syllables and cadences of the name which Pineville spoke.

On and on through the cars, passengers sat and chatted, reading or looking through the windows at the landscape unfolding past their windows, while a tall, hale man, glowing with health and dressed in the uniform of lieutenant in the United States Army, strolled by. Nodding to every gaze, smiling at passengers and tipping his hat with the greatest of courtesy, walking with care to avoid offense or brushing passengers with his sheathed saber, the man who once answered to the name of Lieutenant Anderson Caldwell continued his walk, hollowed out, a mobile shell carrying only an unpronounceable name, cold mocking laughter, and an unbroken howl of anguish behind empty eyes.

Chapter 9

Dust and wind slipped around Aquinas, a chilly shawl stealing the heat of the lodge. His conversation with the two mystical beings had given him, for the first time since the Council handed him his assignment, a deep-rooted sense of fear and unease, coiled in his gut. He concentrated on breathing, a cleansing and circular pattern he learned as a novice magus. The visiting professor, a Buddhist sage known as an expert in Tantric castings, claimed it was a technique for meditation, something Aquinas had yet to master. He understood the point of meditation, but not its practice.

Still, as the moon sank closer to the purpling earth in the nearing dawn, he wished he understood the practice a little better. *The calm of meditation would be a welcome friend right now*, he thought forlornly. Even his subconscious' sardonic musings seemed to have abandoned him, pushed aside by the terrible idea wedged in his mind like a sliver, drawing all attention to the pain of its presence.

A memory of his beloved uncle—tanned and strong from working in the Missouri sun, talking earnestly with a young Aquinas over beer and Latin texts lit by lantern—surfaced in Aquinas' mind, bringing a fleeting smile to the magus. Simon was a learned traveler who returned from studies abroad to raise his orphaned nephew on the family farmstead, and Aquinas wished he could speak to Uncle Simon now, even if just for a few moments. Whatever else Simon learned in his travels, his ability to listen and offer the right words of guidance were the traits Aquinas learned to value most.

Wish you were here now, uncle, Aquinas thought.

"To whom do you pray, Mr. Moore?" said a voice behind Aquinas. Fights the Wind moved like smoke, appearing from nowhere with barely any warning of his arrival. He sat beside Aquinas, sliding easily into a relaxed but attentive posture, facing the point where the sun would soon crawl from its nocturnal rest. Unlike Aquinas, he seemed composed and calm, ready to face whatever was ahead. *His hands don't even shake in the cold*, Aquinas noted.

"My uncle," Aquinas said automatically. The answer surprised him, but it was out now, and what else was prayer but seeking wisdom from the unseen? The truth of it was clear to the magus.

To his surprise, Fights the Wind nodded with approval. "Then you have good sense after all. Those who came before us have wisdom to offer if we only listen. I don't think the white god has much to say to his people."

"Many of his people don't have much to say to magi of any stripe," Aquinas said.

Fights the Wind said nothing for a moment, contemplating the horizon. Finally, the shaman said, "Are we talking about the same white god? The one who cast out demons, healed the sick, raised the dead? He was quite the magus. Not even death or a great rock could hold him back."

Aquinas nodded. "Many of my people think that was just the hand of his father working through him."

"My father's hand works through me at times," Fights the Wind said. "Can I be a white god as well? The water into wine would come in handy now and then."

"There's not much of a future in it," Aquinas said, and laughed. Fights the Wind laughed also, his booming chuckles arrowing out over the land and causing a sleeping dog by a nearby shelter to start. Theological discussions were not usually Aquinas' cup of tea, but it distracted him for a moment. Heresy had not crossed the magus' mind; most magi retaining any belief in Godhead tended toward the idea an infinite being had better things to worry about than whether someone was making jokes in His, Her or Their name.

The two men sat quietly for a space of minutes, watching the sky bleach itself of darkness and stars fade into the lightening blue. Breezes smelling of dew and earth brushed by the men as they blew into camp, and the sound of bodies stirring in some of the lodges to the southeast reached their ears. A small bird darted overhead and to the south, searching for breakfast.

"I had a pair of visitors last night. I didn't catch the man's name, but he called the lady with him Eagle Woman," Aquinas said.

"You were visited by Eagle Woman?" Fights the Wind said, slightly interested now. "That's unusual. I'd expected her to visit my father. Describe her companion."

Aquinas did, mentioning the colors and shadings of the porter's aura; a physical description, he was sure, would have been useless. He related his conversation with the two visitors, and the epiphany he had regarding the overall plan of the mind behind the growing darkness in the dreaming. There was no point in hedging bets with talk of sensing; even those not normally attuned to it could feel it now, oppressive and looming just at the edge of perception. Aquinas was able to forget about it occasionally, sometimes for an hour or two at a time, but it always intruded on his thoughts before too much time passed. How a shaman as powerful and in sympathy with the dreaming as Calls Thunder Song could stand it, Aquinas had no idea, and less desire to find out.

When the magus finished, Fights the Wind stared into the sky where the moon rode most of the night. For all Aquinas could tell, the shaman might have been carved in oak and left to petrify on the prairie. *He must be meditating on what I said*, Aquinas thought. After what seemed an hour, Fights the Wind still had not moved.

"Meditating?" Aquinas said as the sun broke through the horizon.

"That idea of yours is truly monstrous," Fights the Wind said, his voice ringing like struck steel, "and if it wasn't so likely to be true, I would curse you for thinking it."

"If it wasn't so likely to be true, I would never have voiced it," Aquinas said. "I wish it hadn't occurred to me, or that it seems so truthful."

Fights the Wind turned his head to face Aquinas. The emotion in the shaman's now cloud-gray eyes was unmistakable, but unexpected. Rage, hurt, surprise: Aquinas expected every one of those in his friend's eyes and more. He had no idea how to react to the undiluted sorrow he saw in Fights the Wind now.

"This is why we'll soon leave this world," Fights the Wind said. "We can fight the white men until Coyote brings down the sun, but your ideas...we have no defense against those monstrosities. Such thoughts, we cannot abide. I don't know how we would hold them, even if we could create them."

Every human has this inside, Aquinas wanted to say, but history was not on his side, so he said nothing. As he stared at the rising dawn, it occurred to him if they were unable to put a stop to the unknown darkness, it might require equal savagery to fight it, a thought that did nothing to improve his mood.

Golden light filled the sky, turning the violet bowl into a lighter, warmer shade. The magus and the shaman sat facing the dawn, each pondering the world and future they faced. Despite the morning that filled their eyes, all either of them could see was blood and death and the smoke of a thousand fires. Neither one saw the world that lay beyond that vision, but both assumed it would be a dead one.

Chapter 10

Calls Thunder Song sat in the darkened lodge, slivers and picks of light through the roughened log walls his only illumination, as he pondered the medicine wheel etched into the dirt floor. Ritual and will would push him through to the dreaming, perhaps grant him an audience with the Spirit Councils or even Coyote himself, but he had nothing new to offer. If they had something to tell him, they would. Eagle Woman and her companion had a deep and vested interest in keeping the human world alive, and Coyote simply wouldn't want the fun to end. Why they visited the white magus was an intriguing question; he'd sensed their presence in the night, and since his son said nothing to him, it was clear who received their attention. The ancient shaman decided to have a discussion with the magus soon.

In the meantime, there was the dreaming. Sensing and guessing at shadows provided no answers, the shaman knew, so a more direct investigation was needed. Shoshone ritual songs were strong and flexible, but for some aspects of the dreaming, silence was best. Calls Thunder Song cleared his mind of his worries, his surroundings. He closed his eyes and captured the lodge in his memory, now the whole of his universe. Bit by bit, he emptied his mind of the world: the dappled light patterns, the cool solidity of dirt beneath him, the breath in his lungs, the medicine wheel on the floor. Soon, his universe was contracted to only his heartbeat, strong and regular in the featureless void. In his attention, it too faded into nothing, and in the perfect emptiness, the dreaming unfolded.

Calls Thunder Song never tried to describe the dreaming to anyone else; he knew even those who sometimes accompanied him did not see it as he did. For him, the dreaming was like emerging into summer sunlight after a week underground. Light and shadow had razor-sharp edges; smells stung the nose and delighted the palate; sounds enveloped him in a blanket of noise and meaning. The geography was that of his home grounds, but more lush and verdant, far more rich than his world ever was. Entering the dreaming was never difficult. Going back always was.

This time, however, the dreaming did not start by the placid river and meadows of the homeland he knew. Calls Thunder Song found himself in a narrow wood-and-iron box, the long aisle past the door behind him jammed with white people on hard wooden benches, rocking side to side to the rhythmic thrumming of a noise he felt in his bones rather than heard. Turning his head, he saw a great window to his left, flat fields and prairie scrub rolling by as he watched. To his right, a sliding door, low voices in murmured conversation on the other side of its wood grain and brass façade.

Whatever the darkness was, the shaman realized, its source was in the room beyond the sliding door. He could literally see it here, pulsing at the borders of the door like an obsidian heart, throbbing and curdling the air with its presence. He put his left hand on the door lightly, his right reaching for the bone knife he kept clasped to his hip, but did not move to open the door. Fighting in the dreaming was dangerous in numerous ways, and fighting without understanding the enemy was surely suicide. He looked around. It was clear none of the passengers could sense him here; two porters and a conductor passed him by without a glance. Calls Thunder Song leaned slowly into the door and listened.

The conversation was too low at first to be caught, but the shaman breathed deeply and focused on the words, voiding the noise around him just as he cut out the world to enter the dreaming. To his surprise, the focus did not help; he could hear the words now, but the language being spoken was unlike any Calls Thunder Song ever heard, low and sibilant, like snakes given human speech. That was further proof the darkness stemmed from a non-human entity. All human languages were the same in the dreaming, giving any visitor the ability to understand and be understood. The shaman did not know of any non-human languages, other than the First Speech the Spirit Councils only spoke among themselves, but he suspected he was hearing his first.

Whatever the voices were saying, they were excited about it; the hissing rose in pitch, and the words seemed to flow faster and with more emphasis. *The voices are arguing about something,* the shaman thought. *What could darkness be arguing about with itself?*

The shaman placed his palm flat against the door and again stilled his breathing. Listening like this was dangerous, but knowing something, anything about the enemy was important enough to risk discovery. Leaning in, holding his breath, he placed an ear carefully against the wood. Oddly, through the door's reassuring solidity, the hiss and snap of the words resolved themselves to nearly-comprehensible patterns, approaching human speech with slithery speed. Comprehension, almost within his grasp, floated just beyond him as one of the voices read off a list, the words sounding as though they came from a mouth used to having more teeth. *Is it summoning something*, Calls Thunder Song wondered, and a word caught his attention. Shoshone, the voice said. Then it said another word, which sounded like Kiowa.

Tribes, Calls Thunder Song thought. *They're naming tribes. Are these the ones being targeted by whatever these things are working on?*

His breath caught, and the voices beyond the door stopped. One heartbeat passed, and the shaman froze against the door. Vibrations from the train wheels thrummed up into his feet, but beyond those, he felt a minute shifting, the tiniest drop of mystical pressure, and he knew one of the voices within the room was redirecting some force. Instinct dropped him swiftly to the floor with an explosive exhale, a fraction of a second before the top half of the sliding door erupted into slivers and twisted metal fragments, scorching the air with smoke and the tang of something alien. Pushing off with powerful legs, Calls Thunder Song cleared the doorway just before the bottom half of the door exploded outward in the same fashion.

Something stepped out into the hall behind the door's explosion, something with an aura unlike anything Calls Thunder Song had experienced: knotted ropes of force shining in a spiky bilious color that did not, could not exist in the human universe, flowing around a core of clotted necrotic fire that appeared to form a face in the flickering, endlessly leering power surrounding the thing. Every pore of the shaman's skin felt as if they were trying to tear themselves free and run screaming, and the shaman knew he did not want this thing's attention. Coyote granted him a little luck; the thing—which appeared to be wearing a military officer's uniform—had turned to its left when emerging from the room, delaying its spotting the shaman, still on the floor to the thing's right.

A casting was out of the question here; the only course that didn't lead to a fight he was ill-prepared for was retreat. Without taking his eyes from the thing in the uniform, which was beginning to turn toward him, he reached with focused will for the psychic anchor keeping him in the dreaming. The thing continued to turn, its gaze warping the fabric of reality ever so gently as it passed.

Coyote's eyes, this thing has power, Calls Thunder Song thought even as his attention found the link to his anchor and snapped it with a focused blast of adrenaline-punched intention. The dreaming, freed of the tension that kept the shaman in its elusive reality, snapped Calls Thunder Song back into the human plane, mere inches from the edge of the thing's leprous gaze.

In the dreaming, the thing that now wore Colonel McAlister's face and body—another agent from the space between the spheres, a being that also worshiped the First—saw the ripple of something passing and smoothing over, leaving no trace behind. The thing that called itself Pineville had explained that there would be interference from some of the humans that infested this new world, and it appeared one had come to visit. It held out its hand, sensing the faint trace of energy the shaman left, marking the flavor of aura there. When it fully manifested into the physical realm, instead of the fluid half-life between the dreaming and human "reality" the shell afforded it, it would seek out the owner of this aura and devour him slowly. For now, it would wait.

It turned back from the hall, unconcerned with the shrapnel in the hall or the human passengers on the train—a minor incantation from its colleague would disguise the event and its damage in any case—and went back into the room to resume its conversation with the agent called Pineville. There were still many details to discuss, many things to plan, and having eaten soon after it arrived, it wasn't hungry just yet anyway.

Like a gray wave, the world rushed back into Calls Thunder Song's senses, not as bright or clear as the dreaming, but reassuringly solid and quiet after his near-miss on the train. Smells of earth and terror struck him, and he realized his encounter could have been a supreme error. *I know something of them now,* he thought as he breathed deeply, trying to calm his galloping heart, *but what did I reveal? What have I given them to use against us?*

The shaman opened his eyes and took comfort from the dappled logs and dirt of the lodge around him. He looked down at the medicine wheel, at the pictographs of world spirits and trickster gods etched within its boundaries. Its solidity calmed him, and as he looked over the ancient symbols, he realized it was time to seek more assistance. Taking help from the white men, even if it was a token gesture, was straightforward enough for Calls Thunder Song, who didn't care for the politics and machinations of men. Against the things he had seen, aid from a higher source was needed.

He rose from his sitting, old muscles feeling knotted and cramped in the aftermath of adrenaline, and walked into the morning sunshine, light and heat sinking into his skin and chasing the chill away. Calls Thunder Song scanned the area and called to his son and the magus, who were sitting on a small rise on the edge of the camp.

"Come," he said to the men as they approached. "I've been in the dreaming, and seen what we face."

"And?" Aquinas asked as Calls Thunder Song fell silent.

Calls Thunder Song looked at the magus, but it was Fights the Wind who spoke. "My father wishes to speak before the Spirit Councils. He will ask the gods for help."

The old shaman nodded. A burst of pride filled his chest; his son had grown up strong and wise, and would make a fine mystic leader for his tribe. He only hoped Fights the Wind would get the chance to prove to all what his father already knew. "We each have work to do, Mr. Moore. I will prepare the rituals to ask permission and contact them. Fights the Wind, you must prepare the tribes for what is coming."

A flicker of surprise flashed in cloud-gray eyes. "Tribes? Which do you wish me to contact?"

"All of them," Calls Thunder Song said, "even the Lakota. Our differences mean nothing now."

"As you wish, Father," Fights the Wind replied. "The riders will leave this morning. It'll be difficult, though; you know how most of them will react."

"Your task is merely very difficult, my son," Calls Thunder Song said, turning to Aquinas. "The truly difficult task falls to Mr. Moore. I'm afraid I must ask you to slow down the railroad project in whatever way you can, magus."

Aquinas wanted to object, but realized whatever he had to say in the way of excuses was inadequate. The railroad had to be stopped, or at least slowed down to the point that a defense could be made. Even knowing that, however, did not help with the enormity of the task before him. After a long pause, the magus nodded. He knew now, in a primal, gut-deep way he had not understood before, what the Council was up to when they sent him west with such vague instructions and so little oversight.

If it's any consolation, you have made an excellent stalking horse, Uncle Simon's voice echoed in his head. Aquinas didn't find this observation reassuring.

Chapter 11

The scent of copper, heavy and wet, hung in the air, pinned to the screams of the dying and mixing with a spicy bouquet of fear, adrenaline and human voiding. A miasma of death energy coated the interior of the passenger car, ran down the windows and the walls, and pooled on the floor. The thing called Pineville knew it would soak into the wood understructure and framing, might even stain the iron beneath, even though iron was resistant to most magic in this world. Most, but not all.

For now, it was enough to enjoy the bouquet of death and fear, like a gourmand would savor the scent of a feast being prepared. It was a heady mix, and it made him hungry. Ravenous, in fact, but another feeding could wait.

The thing now called McAlister walked back into the room Pineville had reserved and shut the door, regretfully sealing off the carnage stench from the car outside. "Impressive, Pineville, but your lieutenant didn't get as far as I'd hoped. Those deputy marshals toward the dining car brought him down with only 14 shots."

"These bodies aren't as hardy as ours," Pineville agreed, with a touch of a smile about his placid features, "but they taste much better. Besides, he managed to kill seven of the cattle, and I suspect three more will be dead before we reach the next town. That's sufficient. Don't be greedy, McAlister."

McAlister growled softly, a sound that amused Pineville to no end. Although the physical structures of Pineville's and McAlister's original forms were vastly different, they had roughly the same gender divisions, and the thing that wore McAlister had, in the terms of its own universe, originally been female. What difference it made in this world, Pineville did not understand, but it obviously made some difference to McAlister.

"If you like," Pineville said, "we can try and find you an agreeable suit to wear while we're at the work site, one more in keeping with your natural state."

"No," McAlister said, with a barely audible twinge of regret in its voice, "a male suit was the right choice for this world. Females aren't valued here, and having authority of some kind will make the task easier."

Faintly, a gurgling sound, liquid and dark, reached Pineville's ears from the scene of the slaughter just a handful of feet away. Both Pineville and McAlister reached out and sensed the auras of Lieutenant Caldwell's victims; one more had just coughed out a death rattle and added her name (*such a waste of a fine suit*, McAlister thought fleetingly) to Caldwell's tally. A burst of necrotic fire swirled up from the woman's corpse, visible only to the things in their meat suits, and joined the charged atmosphere of thanatopic energy that pulsed and strained against the restraining wards Pineville set before the slaughter began.

"Such potency," McAlister said, half-wonderingly at the flow and hum of death energy around them. "How is it they have such power?"

"Perhaps you can conduct experiments when the Shift is complete," Pineville said. "Exercise that scientific curiosity of yours."

The thought obviously had some draw for McAlister; its eyes warmed at the idea, mind already conjuring up scenes of hundreds of test subjects, strapped into secure restraints and

killed in numerous ways, the eldritch instruments of its home
world measuring the energy flow and nature down to atomic
detail. This world contained millions upon millions of cattle,
McAlister realized, more than enough to explore the issue for
decades to come. With carefully managed breeding programs,
there could easily be enough for perhaps centuries, and seeing
how their young died in similar circumstances might be even
more instructive. The discoveries it could make!

"What a wonderful world," McAlister said, mind swim-
ming with possibilities.

Pineville laughed aloud. "Shall we go?"

McAlister nodded, and Pineville set in motion the complex series of commands and intonations to open a portal to the
railroad work site. McAlister's arrival had renewed Pineville's
impatience to begin work on the project in earnest, and although it took a great deal more power to project one of its
people through cross-space regions in this world—stuck in
the fluidic twilight realm of reality as it was, unable to fully
project itself into this world due to a fundamental quality in
its makeup—it knew a way to generate that power using tools
already at hand, such as the native symbols of the realm. The
latent power within what humans called a pentagram alone
was staggering.

Fortunately, as McAlister observed, the human cattle did
have an immense amount of potential energy within them, and
necromancy was a way of letting it all out at once. A couple
would have been sufficient; every additional death beyond that
just made it easier. If Caldwell had managed to get a little further, Pineville mused, we might have just moved the entire
train.

A thought struck Pineville then, and it paused in its casting. "McAlister, where is Caldwell's body?"

McAlister looked at Pineville for a moment, confused by the question. Then it smiled, a rictus that literally opened the mouth the width of its skull, exposing the gums and teeth to the gaps where wisdom teeth once stood. Pineville made a mental note to have McAlister tone that down. "Toward the back; the surviving deputies shoved his body under the long bench on the south-facing side until they could get back to him, probably to spit on and kick his corpse. You have an idea, it seems."

Pineville shrugged, a boneless gesture that looked serpentine. "Why discard a perfectly good tool? Go and fetch his body back here."

McAlister smiled and cast a quick glamour, disappearing into a muddy shadow to Pineville's human sight. It opened the door and quickly stepped down the hall, relishing the carrion smell and the agonized cries of the wounded as it went. Pineville resumed the casting leisurely, knowing McAlister would be back long before it reached the next place it could pause without compromising the spell work. Within a minute, the glamour-coated McAlister reappeared, the lead-ridden, blood-soaked corpse of Lieutenant Caldwell tucked under its arm like an empty valise. It casually dumped Caldwell's remains on the floor as it pulled the door closed.

Pineville squatted down next to the body, joints cracking as it regarded Caldwell. One of the deputies' slugs had torn a furrow in Caldwell's right cheek, exposing muscle and molar beneath a sheathing of clotted red and black, but his face was otherwise unmarked. Reading the fading energy lines of the body, Pineville saw that if Caldwell were still breathing, he would have suffered immense pain. Virtually every major organ had been pierced by lead at least once, and his ribs and sternum were barely more than splinters. His legs were still whole, as was his left arm, but two fingers were missing from his right hand, and any pressure at all would likely shatter the collarbones, as both had gouges and nicks from the fusillade Caldwell faced. Not that the lieutenant, mind shattered and reeling from his exposure to the First's full name, noticed much.

"If you're going to animate him, you should hurry," McAlister said, watching the thanatopic energy coalesce into half-formed structures in response to Pineville's casting. "There's barely enough there to keep the body in motion."

"Oh, he's not going anywhere," Pineville replied, standing up and turning his attention back to the casting. "In a way, it's too bad he wasn't high enough in the military to use as a suit. He really was quite helpful."

"If we were far enough along that the First could come in, instead of just making His face known--," began McAlister.

"Then we wouldn't need to do this, would we?" replied Pineville. "This project would have been a lot shorter and already be finished, and we could be feeding like royalty, instead of living a half-life in this ridiculous flesh."

McAlister studied Pineville for a moment, the paused casting making a mystic shadow around its head, like an ill-formed halo of smoke and interrupted vision. "I don't remember you being so impatient, Pineville. Perhaps you've been in this realm too long."

Pineville looked down at the body on the floor, cooling as it lay, galaxies of bacteria and microorganisms dying as the flesh continued its slide into biological entropy. *First strike me, am I feeling nostalgic for this meal, this talking entrée of meat and feeble spirit?* "Perhaps, but it won't be this realm for much longer. I'll reanimate him once we get to the work site."

With that, Pineville resumed the casting, the energy flow

of death swirling and forming around it as words and symbols formed a shell of will around the room. To human eyes, there would have been no change, save for perhaps a slight dimming of the light from the windows as the afternoon sun streamed in. However, there were no human eyes in the room, only once-human meat with alien intelligences inside, and they perceived a shifting of space, geometries complex and far beyond human perception or comprehension unfolding and refolding around them. Three dimensions became six, then eleven, then a number with no human analogue, and reality shuddered as the death of eight humans propelled a chunk of spacetime across the skin of the world. With a ripple, normality reasserted itself, and the continued moans and stench of the dying aboard one westbound train resonated inside one particular passenger car, echoing within a now-empty room.

Under the hammering sun, hundreds of men of all races were burning their skin the same color, tanned into uniformity by the blazing Utah heat and the sound of tools striking rock, ringing against metal. A tent city had sprung up, fed by wagon trains and supply lines, and the crawl of exhausted workers and impassive foremen gave the work site a turgid, depressive feel. Soldiers, drained by the heat and burdened beneath oppressive uniforms designed for colder climes, wilted inside their discipline, barely maintaining the illusion of order and control. A weak breeze occasionally intruded, spreading dust and the faint promise of relief around the site.

One tent, near the command post at the center of the nomad city, rippled and shuddered lightly, barely more than the poor desert puffing could account for to a sharp-eyed observer. Had any of the personnel around it been paying attention, they might have sworn the tent was empty, awaiting the delegation from Washington due in four days to oversee the final phase of the project and take back any last-minute news or changes. But there were no attentive eyes on the tent, and thus, the arrival of two beings wearing human skin and bearing a uniformed corpse went unnoticed.

McAlister casually lifted the flap, looking out into the desultory heat and observing the activity around the work site. From a distance, the clang of tools and hand carts sounded like the beatings of an arrhythmic, dying heart. "By the First, this place is a despairing pit. How can you bear to leave it?"

Pineville breathed in deep, absorbing the overlying emotions hungrily. "This is my first time here. There was no need to come to any of the previous work sites, and there was too much to do in Washington. Sadly, killing a number of people in one place in Washington attracts attention, more than I wanted."

"Understood," said McAlister, relishing the heat and space after the gluttony of the train. It turned and looked at Caldwell, now resting on one of the tent's three cots, the patter of slowly leaking blood catching its attention. "We'll have to clean him up if we want him to blend in around here, not to mention getting another uniform."

"First things first," said Pineville, rolling up its sleeves past the elbow. "Hand me that Bowie knife you've got strapped to your hip. Raising him at this point will require a little more than spells."

McAlister passed over the foot-long knife, the steel blade nicked and pitted but still thick and honed to a surgical edge. Pineville took the knife, opened the tattered rags of Caldwell's uniform to expose grey and mottled skin. It spoke a series of extended and thorny phrases, consonants and glottal sounds extending past hearing into ranges of meaning only the meat-suited things could perceive. Only Pineville's mystical ability enabled its human tongue and palate to shape the sounds at all, and as the spell progressed and the casting deepened in power and complexity, blood as black and thick as oil pattered from Pineville's mouth and gums. Finally, as a glistening pool of black formed on Caldwell's cold skin, Pineville began to cut, digging deeply into the rigid skin and muscle.

After a minute, the interior cavity of Caldwell's body was exposed, opening the rotting secrets of his corpse to the sun. *A well-laid table*, Pineville thought as he surveyed the graying organs and scrim of yellowish fat, measuring the fading energies within.

After three minutes, the flesh began to move, jerkily and slowly at first, then with greater ease. Blood, turned black and clotted in his collapsing veins, roiled and flowed until it resembled a thin oil. Beneath Pineville's ministrations, the vestiges of Caldwell's aura began to brighten and knit, regaining strength as the casting progressed.

After four minutes, the reanimated Caldwell began to scream. Anticipating this, Pineville had decided to reanimate the lungs last. Except to talk, Caldwell really didn't need them anymore, and his agonized screaming would have drawn unwanted attention from other officers or workers.

After an additional four minutes, the spell was complete, and the reanimated Caldwell was sitting up, clutching his body as the balky flesh visibly healed the ragged chasm in his chest as he watched. Pineville stood back and admired its work; since Caldwell was still dead, the wounds that killed him wouldn't get any better, but neither would they get any worse, and no heartbeat meant no blood. Strangely, being dead seemed to have restored his reason, as the intelligence that stared out from the ebon pools of Caldwell's eyes was recognizably the lieutenant.

"Hello, Lieutenant," Pineville said as the last traces of Pineville's surgery smoothed over and vanished from the lieutenant's chest. "I have work for you, and if you do your job with your usual imagination and efficiency, there's a substantial reward in it for you."

Caldwell stared at Pineville, his eyes unblinking. He saw clearly now the things residing inside the men once known as Pineville and Colonel McAlister, and wondered how he could have missed the greasy stains they left upon reality. Then again, many things were different now. His reason was still sluggish, but his memories weren't, and he could see the events that led to this point in time. Those events crushed his sanity, turned him into a homicidal automaton, and had resurrected him into a half-life as an ambulatory corpse in the company of creatures more monstrous than anything from the Pit. Demons, Caldwell thought, would have been preferable.

"You killed me," Caldwell finally said, his tongue fat and awkward in his mouth.

"If you would like to be dead again at some point, you'll do as I command you, lieutenant," Pineville said. It casually wiped the Bowie knife clean of Caldwell's blood, nearly as black as Pineville's had been in the sunlight streaming down from the smoke aperture at the tent's peak, and handed the blade back to McAlister, who took the blade and resheathed it, a thoughtful expression on its face. The skin of Pineville's hands, Caldwell noticed without surprise, was absorbing Caldwell's blood as he watched, leaving smooth unlined skin in its wake. "The spell used to reanimate you will keep your consciousness locked to your remains, and your body will rot far slower now than normal. Your sun will go black long before your body releases you."

Caldwell said nothing, his brain turning Pineville's words over and over as he thought. The events of the last few days impressed the depth of Pineville's evil upon him, and while he did not relish the idea of this project coming to pass, he liked the idea of spending eternity rotting even less. Still, some small spark of him rebelled at the thought of doing nothing, and he resolved to wait and play along. His chances for rebellion were small, but as Pineville pointed out, he had nothing left but time. He waited for Pineville to continue, but Pineville said nothing, looking at the lieutenant with an amused and expectant expression. Light, strong and hot, speared down from the circle of blue in the tent's peak overhead, making the gathering shadows at the tent's walls all the stronger.

"Well, Lieutenant? You can speak," Pineville finally said, McAlister standing behind it and appearing to lose interest in the conversation.

"Yes, Mr. Pineville," Caldwell said, letting his slack facial muscles disguise the sudden understanding that struck him like a punch. Whatever horrors Pineville had done to him, it seemed the thing had inadvertently done Caldwell at least one favor. Pineville could no longer read his thoughts, or at the very least, wasn't trying. Perhaps it thought the dead man couldn't have any, or perhaps death rendered his brain impervious to Pineville's reading. It did not matter. For the moment, at least, Caldwell's mind was again his own, and that meant he regained some small advantage.

"Are you going to share this toy, Pineville?" McAlister said, and again, Caldwell's death mask hid his true thoughts. *Perhaps Pineville's resurrection spell has left me other advantages as well*, a new, cold voice said in the lieutenant's mind, a voice he gladly recognized as his own. To be dead and have the monster Pineville's voice in his head, the lieutenant reckoned, would be far more of Hell than he already had, and far more than he could take. He shifted, feeling the gravelly pitch of bone splinters and lead within his body.

"This toy has work to do," Pineville replied. "Make your own if you can find someone of such usefulness, McAlister."

"Ah, but you do such good work," McAlister said, smiling a horrible wide grin. Before his death, Caldwell would have found that terrifying. *Amazing the perspective that dying lends*, the cold voice in his head told him. *Imagine the work someone like Poe might have produced with the same perspective.*

"Flatterer," Pineville said. It turned to face Caldwell again. "Lieutenant, word of your death may or may not have reached the garrison by now, but we'll take no chances. I have another job for you, more of a … well, hands-on type of work."

The lieutenant listened as Pineville outlined its plan to Caldwell, what it wanted of him and how to do it. Caldwell, now stripped of life's comforting illusions and viewing the world with death's cold clarity, understood that Pineville's plan was extremely intelligent, well-thought out and, worst of all, fairly simple at the heart of it. It was likely to work at least in part, no matter what was done, even if the government knew of the plan and worked to stop it. The particulars were too far along, the pieces to come too much in line with the government's goals. If Pineville had been human, the lieutenant would have called him genius.

But nothing is completed yet, that rebellious spark within Caldwell said. *There is still time.* Much to his surprise, Caldwell agreed.

"Understand, Lieutenant?" Pineville said as it finished explaining the plan and Caldwell's role in it. Caldwell nodded; the only hope he had in thwarting Pineville in any way, he saw, lay in playing along until a tipping point was reached.

His part was minor, but it might put him in contact with forces better-equipped to deal with Pineville and McAlister. Whether he could convince those forces of what was happening was another story.

At least they can't kill you, the cold voice said, and he fought back a sudden urge to laugh.

"Lie down and wait for nightfall," Pineville told Caldwell. "Change your uniform before you go. Bullet holes draw questions."

Caldwell nodded and lay down, his mind pondering what he knew about the plans and what little he'd heard of those who might oppose them. *What could I say*, he wondered, *to convince an Indian shaman the end of the world was near?* Somehow, he was sure even being a walking corpse wouldn't be enough argument for such a man, or men, if Pineville was to be believed. He closed his eyes, knowing sleep was likely forever beyond him, and hoped for inspiration to strike.

Chapter 12

Despite his experience with magical travel, especially Calls Thunder Song's facility with the dreaming, Aquinas always felt most comfortable on the back of a horse, feeling the wind stream through his hair, the heat and tension of powerful muscles uncoiling beneath him. Some of the older magi, he knew, refused to travel by any means other than magical, except for the occasional short walk from place to place. Intellectually, Aquinas understood this, but in his heart, he believed that was asking for trouble. The ascendance of technology, and the concomitant increase in using iron, was going to make the world smaller and more difficult to use magic in. Those who depended on magic for their daily lives were going to find those lives ever more circumscribed until they became trapped, unable to function or escape. Change was coming, faster in the last twenty years than in the hundred before that, and it was only going to get faster. In some ways, Aquinas reflected, the time of magic might be drawing to a close, and that might not be such a terrible thing. The end of necromancy, for example, could only be good for humanity.

Aquinas shuddered, and spurred his mount on faster. He'd consulted with the Council's chief librarian through scry-glass before starting off on this leg of his trip, poring through recorded accounts of necromantic spells and discussing the ramifications of his awful epiphany with the librarian, who held a senior post on the Council and was one of the few older magi Aquinas thought of as a friend. Herr Schwarzwulf, as had many magi who came of age before the Renaissance, understood the theoretical underpinnings of necromancy, and comprehended the implications of Aquinas' idea more thoroughly than Aquinas himself.

"The real problem with necromantic generation," Schwarzwulf's gruff voice rumbled, a hint of his lycanthropic ancestors still audible, "is that the energy delivered is exponential in relation to the number of victims. Two people killed may release four times the energy as one person, three people killed may release nine times the energy and so on. Even a mediocre magus could call on tremendous amounts of power through necromancy, which is why the Council banned it outright. So much power in unskilled hands could rend reality like onion paper."

"What about skilled hands?" Aquinas asked. "What could the indiscriminate slaughter of tens, maybe hundreds, of people generate for a skilled necromancer?"

The question silenced Schwarzwulf for a long moment, leaving Aquinas to listen to the faint hiss of the scryglass, cutting a channel through the dreaming (*you think of it in Calls Thunder Song's words now*, Uncle Simon's voice pointed out) to pour out torrents of words. Silence stretched on for over a minute, until the old magus' words came softly back to the conversation.

"Even gods don't wield that much power," said Schwarzwulf. "Not anymore."

Aquinas thanked the magus for his time and cut the connection, pondering what that could mean. Soon after, he asked for a fast horse, and immediately thundered off toward the railroad work site, still half a day's ride away, to do some careful scouting. He knew time was of the essence, but after Calls Thunder Song's experience in the dreaming and Schwarzwulf's implied warning, Aquinas also knew that further exposure to the enemy on such uncertain ground could be fatal. Unless their hands were forced, there could be no direct movement against the enemy until Calls Thunder Song addressed the Spirit Councils anyway. This threat was specifically aimed against the children of Coyote in the short term, and any assistance the wise elder deity could offer was needed.

Fights the Wind also needed time to gather the other tribes to their side, although Aquinas doubted he could gather them all. The Lakota would be particularly difficult to convince. Their shamans were renowned for their power and deep knowledge of the naturalist arts, but were disdainful of other practitioners and had been for centuries. Despite repeated efforts, they hadn't maintained even diplomatic relations with the Council for more than forty years. Little Big Horn and its fallout hadn't helped much, Aquinas reflected. Still, from what he had been able to find, Fights the Wind had a reputation almost as great as his father's, and hopefully that would be enough.

Night began to steal over the earth, and Aquinas scanned the landscape, comparing what he saw with the detailed map Fights the Wind had given him, as well as the composition and color of the meridians in the earth. He was still a span of miles short of the work site, far from the nearest town and unlikely to reach the site before midnight. Despite the spells placed on the horse for speed and nourishment back at the lodge, Aquinas knew the horse was tired, and needed to rest and eat. He slowed the horse's gallop, and looked for a place to dismount and let the horse rest.

The sun's last rays revealed a wide grassy place beside a creek in a shallow valley, and Aquinas allowed the horse to drop to a trot, heading for the water and rich grass it smelled.

His legs sore from tension, Aquinas brought the horse to a halt and swung heavily over the saddle, dropping to the ground. His mount began to munch contentedly on the grass as Aquinas stretched his legs and body, feeling knots loosen and burn as he worked out the strain of hard riding. He reached for the canteen hanging loosely at his hip, and sensed more than heard a shifting in the waist-high reeds that lined the creek bank. At the same time, he felt a stirring in the energy that lay over the placid resting area and realized he'd triggered a trap of some kind.

Fine silver lines sprang into being around the meadow, forming a net in the darkness that would temporarily prevent magic from escaping. It could be broken with some effort—the ward was stable, but had all the solidity of a soap bubble—but Aquinas thought it unlikely he would have the time soon. A handful of dark shapes appeared in the reeds, and Aquinas felt a prickling of energy and danger at his back, a subtle sign he might have missed without the sensory boost of adrenaline in his veins. He spun about, hands already in casting position with a spell at the ready, but the words died on his lips as he came face to face with a corpse in a U.S. Army uniform.

Even in the twilit gloom, the signs of death were unmistakable. Gray skin, shining nearly white under the faint moon's glow, made the man's drawn face appear as if it were beginning to slide from his skull. Only the torn belt of skin along the cheek, exposing ivory teeth beneath black shreds of muscle, appeared solid in the argent light. The man's movements were stiff and halting, and the ripe smell of death seized Aquinas' attention, watering his eyes. Oddly, the man's aura was wan and muted, but essentially healthy. A small part of Aquinas' mind questioned this even as the magus reached into his saddlebag for the backup weapon Fights the Wind had insisted he take.

"Where magic fails," the shaman had told him in a serious tone, "metal can prevail."

Free from the specially woven saddlebag's mystic protections, the Colt revolver seemed to drink in the light, forming a shape darker than the night in Aquinas' hand. The sting of cold iron's presence needled his hand even through the ivory grip, but his hand was steady as he drew a bead on the corpse's head. The corpse stopped and jerked its hands up to head height. Brushing back the military-issue wide brim hat, it attempted a smile. The sight made Aquinas queasy.

"It's not me you should worry about," the corpse said haltingly, shadows flickering through the gouge in its cheek as it spoke. A waft of the grave reached the magus, and his dinner rose in his throat.

A rushing feeling, like air escaping a stuffy room through an opened window, tingled across Aquinas' skin. The sensation of power being gathered was unmistakable. Before his consciousness could identify the source, Aquinas was in motion, slapping his horse forward while diving behind it to the right of the corpse. Ozone sizzled, and an arc of electric red power blasted through the spot where Aquinas' skull had been instants before. Before he hit the ground, another arc blasted close behind, missing him by less than two feet. The Colt was still in his hand; despite the cold iron warning in his bones, he raised the pistol and loosed two slugs at the origin of the red arcs.

In response, a fusillade of bright power, striking and beautiful in the darkness, rained out at him from the reeds and shadows by the creekside trees. Smoke and acrid discharge tainted the air, covering the clean scent of water and grass. His horse ran into the darkness, neighing wildly. *There goes my hope of escape,* Aquinas thought, and shot again into the moving shades around him. One of the shapes marching in the dark twisted to one side but continued on. The coppery odor of blood joined the other smells, giving the stench a texture thick enough to hang pictures on.

The moonlight and faint illumination of the ward was no longer enough for Aquinas to see by in the deepening night, and his options seemed to be short. The uniformed corpse had not moved any further, but the other shadows were progressing toward him, and a sense of bloodlust and predatory hunger reached his mystic sensing. He looked up at the ward overhead; still there, pale and resilient in the night. Such a ward, he thought, can't be rigid; it's too weak.

Magi training in the Council was rigorous in many aspects, and defensive strategies had been one of the most intensive of those; several plans and possibilities flickered through Aquinas' memories, and he quickly found one that might work. The shapes were drawing nearer, and had foolishly bunched up close to each other. Their own wards looked obsidian and edged, ready for frontal assaults, but Aquinas had a different approach in mind. Quickly, he shoved the Colt into his pants, and with his left hand, he made a choppy runesign. In his right hand, a fireball bloomed, orange fury flaring from the ball and licking harmlessly at his fingers. Aquinas yelled, "Catch!" and threw the fireball straight into the air in a powerful underarm throw. As he expected, the ball flew straight into the ward high overhead, stretched the restraining lines, and was ejected downward, following the angle he'd roughly calculated.

The shapes looked up, as he'd expected, in time to see the fireball bounced down into their midst and splash into drops and sheets of twisting flame around them. The shapes immediately caught fire, scorching the grass and the lowest leaves on the trees as their eldritch bodies burned brightly, the sorcery of their forms igniting in the rush of mystic power. Howling and agonized screeching filled Aquinas' ears, but the fire claimed them quickly, and within seconds, the shapes were ash and cinders.

Whirling, Aquinas drew the Colt from his waist and brought the gun to bear on the uniformed corpse, who hadn't moved since Aquinas first drew on it. Its hands were still up, and though the flicker of the firelight and the dark slash of a ruined cheek made it hard to discern, Aquinas thought he saw the corpse smile briefly. The ward shimmered around him but held for the moment.

"Probably shouldn't have used such flammable help," Aquinas said slowly.

"They served their purpose," the corpse said, clearer but still with difficulty. "It was as effective as needed."

"Oh?" Aquinas said, quickly spreading his perception over a wider area. Other than himself and the uniformed dead man, no other sentient creature was anywhere within the ward. Of course, Aquinas reflected, outside the ward there could be a battalion of lycanthropes backed by any number of troubles: necromancers, demons, Pinkertons.

"Allow me," the corpse said, and waved a hand in a stiff but recognizable runesign. A sense of pressure, the shimmer of gossamer unraveling, and the ward was gone. Aquinas' senses expanded as far as he could reach, but picked up nothing.

Tingling and heavy, the gun remained trained on the dead man. Aquinas looked at the corpse and said, "All right. You've got my attention, dead man."

The corpse shuddered, a flicker of distaste making the teeth in his ruined cheek click and chatter. Nausea coiled a little more in Aquinas' gut. "I was killed and brought back to this half-life by a monster with an unholy plan. I was told someone would be coming along this path who was a danger to this plan, though I was expecting an Indian."

"A necromancer did this," Aquinas said aloud.

The dead man shook his head. "Not in the sense you mean. This person wears a human like clothing, but he's not of this world, nor any world I'd visit."

Aquinas frowned, but an idea clutched at his chest. If this darkness wasn't even human…" Were you raised through necromancy?"

"I'm not sure, but that seems close enough," the corpse shrugged. "Whatever the magic used, the thing that did this to me is potent with it, and other forces. It's taken over the identity of an official with the federal government, and has been manipulating railroad construction in order to create a great steel design."

What? Aquinas stared at the dead man, utterly confused. "What does that have to do with the aboriginal tribes? A local shaman has uncovered an immense threat to all the Indian tribes, something likely involving necromancy."

"That's another part of this monster's plan," the corpse said. "He intends to finish the railroad, and use contacts in the military to launch a full-scale attack against the Indian tribes. The resulting carnage—"

"—would power a massive necromantic casting," Aquinas finished, nape crawling as he contemplated the scope of the plan. "Which tribes will be attacked?"

"All of them in the West, if he can," the corpse said.

Silence, cold and still, followed the corpse's words. Aquinas looked at the dead man, who returned his gaze. *The news continues to improve,* his subconscious told him, no longer jocular. *Even the Council might not be enough,* Aquinas thought in return.

"What's the point of all this?" Aquinas asked. At that moment, had Fights the Wind or Uncle Simon or anyone else appeared to him and asked him what he hoped for, Aquinas couldn't have answered. Horror is easy enough to deal with for a trained magus; each one faces their own personal fears and demons as part of training. What this plan was propelled by wasn't horror, or power, or any of the other motivations Aquinas understood intellectually. This monstrosity was grander, almost theological in scope. The very idea cast doubts on his worldview, and the knowledge of this made him tremble inwardly; he understood now what Fights the Wind felt. Still, he had to know.

"What's this monstrous being trying to accomplish?" Aquinas asked the dead man.

The dead man looked at Aquinas for a long moment, his eyes the only sign of life as the corpse pondered the question. Aquinas noticed, with some detachment, that he had yet to see the soldier breathe, more proof of what his senses told him. Having a conversation with a dead man is not a common occurrence within magi circles, but it wasn't so rare that Aquinas was unnerved by the plain fact of it. He simply never expected to have such a face-to-face encounter.

Finally, the dead man spoke. "The …creature coined a word to describe this plan's purpose. He said it was a concept humans might have eventually discovered. I hope that's not true."

"Did he explain it to you?" Aquinas asked.

The corpse jerked, a short bark rolling from his throat. It took Aquinas a moment to understand the dead man had laughed, short and bitterly. "In exquisite detail. He took great joy in seeing how I took his news, his plans for using the death energy of hundreds of murdered Indians to alter reality. I think he enjoyed that more than he did driving me insane, or resurrecting me into this shell."

"So you understand the plan's purpose," Aquinas said.

The dead man laughed once more, meeting Aquinas' eyes. "He called it worldmaking. He plans to use death energy to alter our world completely, to change the laws of our universe. He intends to make our world more hospitable to the life from his sphere or universe, whatever you want to call it."

Aquinas gasped, and the dead man stumbled forward and clasped the magus' shoulders, drawing him closer. Within a foot of the dead man, the stench was almost visible in its rotted thickness. "And once the worldmaking is complete and our reality is fit for their kind, they and their gods will be moving in."

"They like it here, you see. There's plenty of food."

Chapter 13

Every ritual for the invocation of gods has a section specifically for purification, for making oneself worthy to be seen directly by the deities in question, or at least not offending them with
one's human hygiene. Depending on the god, this cleansing
might be a somewhat casual thing, or a minutely detailed set
of steps to be followed with no deviation. With Coyote and
the Spirit Councils—for one could not be invoked without the
other, not by mere humans anyway—it required a certain level
of attention. Calls Thunder Song, who was widely considered
to have a close relationship with the divine joker of the sky (at
least, as close a relationship as a mortal could possibly have),
made sure he took all the steps needed to keep this relationship.
It wasn't so much that Coyote could or would feel any obliga-
tion, as much as it was establishing a precedent for Coyote to
follow. In human terms, Coyote could be lazy.

Thus, with the utmost attention, Calls Thunder Song began the purification rite, submersing his age-hardened body in
the stream-fed pond near his lodge. Three times, he dropped
into the cold pressure of the water, his breath catching each
time as he emerged into the hot sunlight, air as cold as the
water he'd just left. Three times, he spoke the required words,
a couplet of powerful invocations to Coyote and his brethren.
And, after the steps required by ritual, he performed them an
extra time, showing obeisance specifically to the laughing
sky spirit who created his people through seduction of a dark
beauty whose name was never mentioned in any of the ancient

songs and sagas. Calls Thunder Song suspected it had been Eagle Woman, but it would have been rude to ask.

The first of the rituals complete, the wizened but strong shaman turned to walk up the bank and dress himself again, and there was Coyote, lying flat on his back on Calls Thunder Song's clothes while calmly admiring the morning sky. Sometimes, Coyote liked to appear as other people, disguise himself and see how long it took Calls Thunder Song to figure out it was really him. Today, however, he appeared as Calls Thunder Song himself, an exact duplicate down to the water dripping from his gray braid, except for the luxuriously blond handlebar mustache that rested incongruously under his double's nose, just like that moron Custer's. Coyote's sense of humor was often surpassingly strange.

"Hello, my son," Coyote said, shaking pond water from his hands as he stood.

Calls Thunder Song bowed in respect, but said nothing. Coyote sometimes appeared without being asked, but those appearances weren't always good news. Being a shaman wasn't all magic and ritual; it required being able to read people, and that was one of Calls Thunder Song's greatest skills. Coyote, however, was not people. The shaman was not exactly prepared for this.

"You were planning on speaking to the Spirit Councils today," Coyote said. He reached down, shook the dirt and grass from the shaman's clothes in one snapping motion, and handed them to Calls Thunder Song. "Thought I'd save you the trip."

"You know why I wanted to speak to the assembly?" Calls Thunder Song said, drying himself quickly and dressing.

Coyote laughed lightly. "Did you think you picked up on something that we did not? That I did not?"

"No, Coyote," Calls Thunder Song said. "I am concerned,

though. The dreaming did not reveal to me any inkling of the action the Spirit Councils were taking."

Coyote sighed, and in that moment, the shaman saw everything he feared begin to take shape. "Can't see what isn't there, no matter how hard you look. The Spirit Councils have reviewed the matter and decided that regardless of what happens here, it is long overdue for our people to move past this world. We will migrate through the dreaming into the High Prairies, and take up homes there."

To his credit, Calls Thunder Song did not immediately shout the first profanity that came to mind. Nor did he shout the second. By the time he had reached the eighth or ninth in his mental list, he had calmed sufficiently to sound merely agitated. "So we simply run away? Not all of our people can move through the dreaming. Do we leave them here, to face whatever is done? Are we to abandon this world?"

"This world has already abandoned our people. You've known this for many years. This darkness simply changes the timetable."

Coyote brushed off the seat of his hide pants, chapped and worn from centuries of hunting and playing pranks, and ambled toward the lodge. Calls Thunder Song fell into step beside him, unsurprised to note he couldn't see a single soul moving besides Coyote and himself. Whether Coyote had stopped time, or simply moved the tribe somewhere else while they spoke, he couldn't say. The withdrawal of the Spirit Councils did not entirely surprise him, but he knew Coyote, for all his faults and foibles, loved his people deeply. It was not in the laughing god's nature to shy from a fight, although he was more apt to fool his opponent out of battle than face off in a direct attack. A slim ray of hope pierced Calls Thunder Song's heart; perhaps, he thought, that was Coyote's plan.

The transition into the dreaming was so quick Calls Thunder Song barely noticed it. He opened his mouth to ask Coyote what was happening and closed it as the sight of the High Prairies unfolded before him. Under a sky the color of the sea, a verdant plain stretched for centuries before him. To the northeast, a wooded throng of massive firs and pines grew into a quilt of green and brown that sprawled against jagged mountains, bare and toothed against the marbled sky. A wide ribbon of water wound across the prairie's width, dropping from a thundering tract at one barely-visible side to the rolling breakers of an ocean at the prairie's other side. Herds of bison and horses dotted the landscape, stretches of hoofed thunder-clouds fallen rumbling to earth. Calls Thunder Song knew that his people could march in every direction forever and never run out of world to love and explore. The High Prairies held enough territory for any number of gods and people, even the rapacious whites.

"This will be our new home," Coyote said quietly. "This is the world our people should have always had."

The old shaman stared out at the vision before him, imagining the lives his people, his children could have there, free of the lower world he could even now feel slipping away from him as he fought to keep hold. Without straining, he saw at least four different places where a tribe could settle forever, grow strong and wise at peace with the world. Everything he could want for his people was there.

But not all of his people could be there. He turned back to Coyote.

"All this would cost us is a few lives," said Calls Thunder Song softly. "A few of the Shoshone or the other tribes who can't travel between spaces, the whites with their technology and guns, anyone else not of the people. Nothing we can't replace. Is this so?"

Coyote said nothing. Calls Thunder Song turned to face the trickster spirit, still looking over the vista. His expression was unreadable to the shaman.

"This world is a wonder to behold, but all we'll ever see is blood if we don't try to defend the lower world," Calls Thunder Song finally said.

"This world is a safe one," Coyote said.

"For now," Calls Thunder Song replied. "Besides, if we don't try and defend our people, the power unleashed by the darkness may come to threaten even the High Prairies."

In the vista before them, the sun, brilliant glass in a liquid blue sky, slipped behind a stretch of thundercloud, passing a shadow across the land. The shadow darkened Calls Thunder Song's vision for a moment, and in the sudden quiet before the wind changed, Coyote said, "Do you think the darkness can overcome even the gods in their stronghold?"

"If the gods refuse to fight, it doesn't matter where they're confronted," Calls Thunder Song replied. "They may be defeated without ever taking arms."

"Take care where you go with this," Coyote told the shaman, eyes glinting visibly in the murky shadow. "I hear an accusation in your voice, shaman. Even my forbearance has limits."

Calls Thunder Song wondered what more he could say without drawing the wrath of Coyote upon him. If the great trickster felt insulted, it could go poorly for him, and he might not be able to add his voice to those standing against the dark. Calls Thunder Song did not know if he would be a tipping point, but he knew his power was greater than most, and he could not bear the thought of not defending his world, his people.

That is why I must not bandy words, the shaman told

himself. *If Coyote is offended, I will pay for that, but perhaps later. Even in his anger, he likes a good banter.*

"Yes, you hear an accusation," Calls Thunder Song finally said. "My son and a white magus stand ready to defend the people. What does that say, father Coyote, when a white will stand and fight where the gods will not?"

The wind stopped, as did the faint sounds of hooves and whinnies from the High Prairie. Clouds halted, waves ceased to break; it was as if the world beyond the dreaming had shifted, from a beautiful reality to a picture fit for a wall. Earth rippled beneath him, as though he were sitting in a canoe on a restless lake. *Those might have been my last words*, Calls Thunder Song thought, *but so be it.* He turned his attention to Coyote's eyes, two glistening depths of infinity in a mirror of his own face, now slightly ominous with an otherworldly inflection. Unbowed, he met Coyote's gaze with his own level stare.

The first space between heartbeats crawled by in what felt like days. The second went on for what might have been weeks. Calls Thunder Song could feel the tug of sun and moon as he waited for Coyote's reaction, waited for wrath or laughter, he wasn't sure which. He considered all his arguments, all the goodwill he had earned, wondering if it would save him if Coyote decided to take offense. *At least Fights the Wind is in place to take up the mantle should I end up river mud or turned into a chipmunk*, the shaman thought.

"Your shaman has never lacked for bravery," a steely woman's voice said behind Coyote, "and that must count for something."

Coyote did not move, but Calls Thunder Song felt a shift in tension, and he realized the contest of wills was postponed for the moment. It was too much to hope Coyote would consider it done. As Coyote turned, the shaman shifted his gaze to see the edged beauty of Eagle Woman standing bemusedly behind the great trickster, an unassuming Negro male grinning broadly at her side. The man was dressed in a railroad uniform, and Calls Thunder Song realized this must be the porter Aquinas mentioned. Something about him, some aspect of his being seemed familiar, but Calls Thunder Song couldn't place it at first, until the porter tipped him a quick and jovial wink. Then the shaman had it; the porter had Coyote's eyes. Another trickster.

"Eagle Woman," Coyote said. His eyes narrowed at the porter. "Iktomi." A subtle hint of ozone reached Calls Thunder Song, and the faint crackle of electricity, though Coyote didn't move or threaten. *First me, then Iktomi*, the shaman thought. *I may have saved my soul a trip if Coyote loses his temper.*

"Brother," the spider deity in the porter uniform said, "Calls Thunder Song is right, and you know it."

"The Spirit Councils don't agree," Coyote said.

"Why are you agreeing with them?" Eagle Woman asked. "That isn't your style."

"I find nothing funny about this," Coyote said. "No opportunity for tricks, no game to be had." Coyote turned back to face Calls Thunder Song, who hadn't moved a fraction since his eyes locked gazes with Coyote's. "You told me it doesn't matter where the confrontation is if the gods don't fight, and you were right. The Councils have decided this isn't a fight for us; more to the point, it isn't a fight they believe we can win."

Coyote sighed, an exhalation with a whisper of forever in it. Hearing it, Calls Thunder Song knew for a fleeting instant what it was to be ancient beyond the counting of years. The melancholy pressure passed, but it left a chill nestled inside his soul. "In truth, I believe the Councils are right. This darkness is strong and hungry beyond all reason. I've never felt its like. We don't know how to fight it, and we've seen what happens when fighting continues in the face of superior forces we do not understand."

"We change tactics," Eagle Woman said shortly. "Our people adapted to firearms well enough."

"Would you have our people adopt the ways of darkness?" Coyote softly asked. "Should Calls Thunder Song take up teaching necromancy to his son, and the younger shamans of the tribe? Perhaps they can take up skin suits as well. There are enough tribes after all, and plenty of white people who won't be missed."

"That won't be needed," Iktomi said, stepping forward as if to comfort Coyote. "There are other ways to fight them."

"Perhaps," Coyote said, "but they aren't our ways. Our people already suffer from the white ways of thinking and doing. The world has changed, and our people have suffered. Sometimes, change is not the right path."

"So, we let them die?" Eagle Woman said.

"We know what will happen," Coyote said forlornly. "We can save most."

"But you can't guarantee that," Calls Thunder Song said. "There's no way of keeping the High Prairies hidden from the dreaming, as long as—"

All three of the deities looked at Calls Thunder Song as his words came to a complete stop. Like a daydream, or the sudden solution to a problem that's troubled the mind for days, the answer came to the shaman whole and complete, lighting up his mind with its terrible rightness. He understood now what Coyote left unsaid in their earlier conversation, and why the High Prairies would make the perfect home for his people in their gods' eyes.

"It's not enough to retreat through the dreaming, is it?" Calls Thunder Song asked. His heart turned to lead at his words. "You intend to sever the High Prairies from the dreaming, isolate the lower world from the sacred grounds forever."

Coyote said nothing. The trickster god lowered his gaze to the ground thoughtfully, silently. Faintly, the sounds of a thousand hooves trampling rich dirt into clouds of fine dust reached their ears, but Calls Thunder Song no longer thought them welcome. *My people have been all but abandoned,* Calls Thunder Song thought, *and I will find no help here.* With the gods gone, there wouldn't even be an afterworld to join after dying in the battle against the darkness.

Time to go back to my world and do what I can.

"I see," the shaman said aloud. He could think of nothing more to say, no words to tie up his years of service and his relationship to the gods with any meaning, and so he settled for silence. He raised his right hand in farewell, and began the casting through the dreaming with a wordless gesture. Ritual required a formal request to depart, but Calls Thunder Song knew whatever Coyote could possibly do to him for the offense, it would be no worse than the fate to which the gods had abandoned his people.

With only the barest hint of contempt, Calls Thunder Song turned his back on his deities, cast a spellway lighting his path through the ever more obsidian dreaming, and left for the lower world. *Maybe it's time to offer a prayer to the white god,* the shaman thought sardonically as he passed into the in-between. *He certainly can't fail any worse than mine have.*

Chapter 14

"Another white man," Fights the Wind said, his left eyebrow quirked up, "and this time, he comes to me already killed. Perhaps you are Coyote in disguise, and have chosen a spectacularly inappropriate time for a joke."

Oh, if that were true, Aquinas reflected. Every bit of news they received made the threat more dangerous and likely to destroy them all, and here the tribe's one outside ally had brought a walking, talking corpse in a U.S. Army uniform. In the close air of the lodge, the smell of death hung like smoke about the body, which was standing alertly and facing the shaman with an expression of neutral evaluation. Even the French *eau de toilette* one of the braves had surprisingly produced, which Aquinas splashed liberally on and about Lieutenant Caldwell, had done little to disguise his resurrected nature. Fortunately, his gray pallor had receded somewhat. The former Army lieutenant now merely looked pale as a starched bed sheet.

"I wish this was amusing," Aquinas said, "or that what Lieutenant Caldwell has to relate was the setup to an involved prank. Lieutenant?"

The dead man began to speak, outlining in terse sentences the full reach of the plan Pineville had set in motion: the steel design upon the earth, the Tenth Cavalry under the newly absorbed Colonel McAlister, the massive spell powered by the dying of hundreds or thousands of Indians, all of it. Though Aquinas had already heard it all, the light-headed sensation of the earth tilting beneath him returned. He sensed his subconscious seeking different outcomes, hoping against sense everything Lieutenant Caldwell said was wrong, even as he struggled to understand the depths of the mortal danger they faced.

Lieutenant Caldwell finished his explanation, and Aquinas opened his mouth to speak, but Fights the Wind held up a hand. His ruddy skin had turned a pale green, but whether from Caldwell's words or the stench of his decay, Aquinas was unsure. The shaman lowered his head and took three deep, slow breaths. For a moment, he kept his head low, visibly struggling with nausea. Then he straightened up, and from his expression, someone might have just announced a hunting trip was rained out. Aquinas, whose composure was still reeling, envied the shaman his poise, even if it was just a show for the whites.

"We must wait," Fights the Wind finally said, "until my father returns from the Spirit Councils. Until we hear what he has to say, we can make no plans."

Both Aquinas and the dead man nodded. Whatever help the gods could provide might make a substantial difference, particularly with Coyote in their corner. The trickster god was one of the prime movers in most aboriginal American theologies, and when in his milieu, his power was limited only by his fertile imagination. Considering the forces massed against them, a god's intervention might be all that saved them, Aquinas thought.

Fights the Wind said something to Lieutenant Caldwell, his voice too low for the magus to hear. Caldwell shrugged and replied in a voice equally low. The shaman nodded once, and walked toward the lodge door. As he strode past Aquinas, he jerked his head toward the door without losing step and walked into the late afternoon sunshine. Aquinas followed Fights the Wind outside and toward the pond used for ritual cleansings. A soft breeze skipped off the water's surface, cutting the brazen heat of the day with a trace of cool air. A hawk soared in the milky blue vault overhead.

"What in the Christian Hell were you thinking, magus?" Fights the Wind said calmly as they stopped by the pond. Aquinas was taken aback only a little. He expected this reaction, and didn't blame the shaman for it. It had taken long thought before he decided to allow the lieutenant into the camp, and Aquinas was still on his guard around the dead man. "You allowed a possible spy into our midst."

"A calculated risk," Aquinas answered. "Even if he's lying through his teeth, what he says can still be useful to us. Plus, he offered me assistance where it would not have done him any good. There were better ways to make my acquaintance and work his way into our camp. I believe he is true."

"Even so," the shaman argued, "he may not be in control of what he tells the enemy. A reanimated corpse is an unknown when considering self-control or motivation. He could be reporting back to this Mr. Pineville as we speak."

"Perhaps, but that isn't the sense I get," Aquinas said. "Have you or your father raised the dead? I understand it is complex and difficult at best. Very few in the Western Council have attempted it outside the confines of a laboratory."

"Raising the dead is difficult, but not unusually so. Giving them independent will, as this lieutenant seems to have, is much harder and not a good idea. The dead don't think as the living do."

Reality shimmered, rippling the air and earth around them and making Aquinas forget what he was about to say. A thinning of the world appeared, a flat oval of nothing that stretched the air and distorted the view beyond it, and Calls Thunder Song stepped into view without looking behind. He strode out of the dreaming, reality bouncing and solidifying in his wake, and without a word walked toward his lodge, eyes fixed on the path before him. Fights the Wind called his name, but the old shaman gave no sign of hearing, continuing his march toward the lodge. The disquiet in Fights the Wind's eyes didn't reassure Aquinas.

"Wait here," Fights the Wind said, and ran after his father, calling his name as he raced to catch up. Calls Thunder Song reached his lodge and ducked inside, followed closely by Fights the Wind. Aquinas wondered how the old shaman would react to the dead man wearing a U.S. Army uniform, when he sensed a pressure change at his elbow. Already on edge, Aquinas called on a defensive hex before his sense kicked in, and had cast it before he realized it was only the lieutenant. Before he could recall the casting, Caldwell made a stiff but quick gesture, and the hex deflected into the air to scatter in a thin cloud of smoke. The hex was not without effect; Aquinas saw scoring on the tattered blue cloth of the lieutenant's jacket sleeve, and the graying flesh below suffered the same.

"Are you always this edgy, magus?" Caldwell asked.

"Only when the dead sneak up on me, lieutenant," Aquinas said, struggling to simultaneously keep his nerves and temper in check. He frowned. "How did you get out of the lodge without me seeing you?"

The lieutenant's face gave nothing away, but his eyes seemed a fraction more bemused. "I walked out behind you and simply went in a different direction. You weren't exactly looking around for me."

"That's not the kind of behavior that will gain you trust," Aquinas said.

"I'm a resurrected corpse wearing the uniform of an army seeking to wipe these people off the planet," Caldwell said. "Trust won't be easy to come by anyway. Besides, it seemed prudent to be elsewhere. Did you read Calls Thunder Song's aura?"

Aquinas had not, and said so. Caldwell shook his head. "I don't know what the Spirit Councils told him, but whatever they said, it wasn't what he expected. He is not a happy man. Worse, what I saw in his energy looked like despair."

"That seems unlikely," Aquinas said. "He has the ear of the gods."

At that moment, Fights the Wind walked out of the lodge, slowly and haltingly. Aquinas was close enough to read his face, the pale green tinge of his skin. Reading Fights the Wind's aura was redundant, but from the waves of soul sickness and despair that came off the medicine lodge like heat, Aquinas knew Lieutenant Caldwell's assertion was correct. The only news that could make Calls Thunder Song react in such a way was the total cessation of hope. Coyote had refused the great shaman's entreaties. There would be no help from the gods of the Spirit Councils against the darkness encroaching.

New moon was high overhead, shining down on the near-silent camp, before either of the shamans was able to speak individually to Aquinas again. He'd cautiously approached Mangas and White Hawk separately to gauge the situation, but neither elder was much help. Mangas looked sorrowful and said something about resting; White Hawk simply snorted disdainfully and walked away, the nicked blade of his war hatchet gleaming balefully in the bleeding sunset. Caldwell had withdrawn to the gentle hillock on the other side of the lodge, far away from the tribal camp and hidden to anyone casually looking in that direction. Aquinas appreciated Caldwell's situation, but did not know what use he could be in the coming battle.

No battle here, the cold voice in his head echoed. *More slaughter, regardless of how the tribes face the cavalry.*

A cold, humorless chuckle bubbled up to his lips and died in his throat. Pineville's plan was brilliant in more aspects than any of them dreamed, for it was only in discussing the options upon Calls Thunder Song's return from the Spirit Councils that the true nature of the trap was laid before them. Why none of them had seen it before, Aquinas could not guess, but it took the least experienced of the elders in magic or warfare to see the hidden blade in Pineville's stratagems.

"The Spirit Councils have turned their backs to us," Calls Thunder Song said in the hurriedly called elder meeting, just as dusk settled into its purple cradle. "I cannot swear that Iktomi and Eagle Woman will stay out of the fray, but we can't count on any of the gods aiding us, even Coyote. Their plan is to withdraw to the High Prairies and cut the path through the dreaming, isolating this world from the sacred grounds forever."

There had been much shouting and disagreement at this point.

"Not all of our people can travel in the dreaming," Many Voices said, eyes wide in horror. "We can't leave our people to face this."

"Yet withdrawal may be our only option," White Hawk said. "Even if we must leave a few behind, our people will be safe with the gods in the High Prairies, free from the darkness and the threat of the whites."

"Abandon our brethren? We can't consider that," Fights the Wind said.

"Abandon a few, save the tribe. Abandon none, we all die," said White Hawk.

"More than a few are unable to travel the dreaming," Loup-Garou said. "We can't spare that many bodies."

"And it won't matter," Mangas said unexpectedly, surprising the other elders. "Whatever option we choose, the darkness wins."

"What do you mean, Mangas?" Loup-Garou asked. "If we take most of our people into the High Prairies, they cannot be exterminated. Our people will triumph."

"But extermination is not the main purpose," Mangas replied. "As I understand it, the darkness the dead man describes wants to use death energy to power a huge spell using a great steel design."

Calls Thunder Song and the other elders nodded.

"If we take our people except for those who can't travel the dreaming, they are left unprotected, and will be slaughtered, thus powering the spell," Mangas said. "If we bid them fight, they will likely be slaughtered in the struggle, and thus power the spell. If they fight and somehow succeed in their battle against the Army, then many soldiers will die, thus powering the spell." The elder looked around the fire at his friends. "Thus do we bring about the end: of our people, the whites and all the other races of the Earth."

Though it was yet another manifestation of the doom facing them, Aquinas felt a glimmer of admiration for Pineville and his planning skills. To work out a plan for mass murder, and simultaneously get an enemy to not only agree to it, but actually build it, took tremendous inspiration. Although Aquinas was no longer a churchgoer, he still remembered some of the things he'd learned over the years, and he had no lingering doubt about the ultimate source for these plans, regardless of whatever it might call itself.

Calls Thunder Song immediately called the meeting closed, ordering the elders and Aquinas to get some rest and rethink the options before them as Calls Thunder Song and

Fights the Wind discussed the tribe's options. *It shouldn't take long*, Aquinas thought ruefully as he watched the stars come out to dance in the night breezes. *Essentially, we're all going to end up dead, be one giant tribe of the deceased, just like—*

Looking up at the constellations, Aquinas felt the stirrings of an idea take hold in his tired brain. The memory of his conversation with Fights the Wind was the seed, and now of all times, with sleep beckoning him and the weight of all humanity on him and his compatriots, a possibility came to light. Of all the options discussed, and all the negative consequences that could result, there was one option that hadn't been touched on, one way to counteract, at least in part, the necromantic spell. As an additional feature, it could be used as a delaying tactic, depending on where and how soon it was deployed. The fact that it was distasteful at best, if not outright illegal and insanely dangerous in the eyes of the Council, had little bearing at the moment.

"We already have the perfect general," Aquinas said aloud, and turned his gaze toward the hidden place where Lieutenant Caldwell sat.

Chapter 15

To their credit, none of the elders immediately cursed upon hearing Aquinas' hastily conceived plan. Smoke curled around the posts and the ceiling, slowly filling the lodge with the rich smell of pine and ash, but no one moved to open the lodge to the evening air. Even Many Voices, the gentle bard of the elders, seemed nonplussed by the proposal Aquinas set forth in his breathless speech after quickly reconvening the elders. The magus hoped it was because they were seriously pondering his idea, and not because they were weighing sending him to the Council in a coffin.

"It has the benefit of being…unexpected," Calls Thunder Song said at last, breaking the stony silence of the meeting. From his expression, the old shaman didn't like the idea much, but compared to the anguished silence he had been imprisoned in since his meeting with the Spirit Councils, even this was an improvement to Aquinas.

"Unexpected?" White Hawk said. "Obscene is a better word. Have you gone mad, magus? How dare you even suggest such a thing?"

"It doesn't call for necromancy of our own," Aquinas said, aware of how precarious his position was among the elders. Even Fights the Wind appeared discomfited, and Aquinas wasn't sure he could count on support from his new friend. For the first time since he arrived, he was keenly aware of being the only white man in the area other than the reanimated body of Lieutenant Caldwell, an association that wasn't a help.

"The spell for resurrection is a straightforward one among the Council's adherents. There's no trafficking with dark forces involved."

"The fact you can say that in all seriousness tells us something deeply disturbing about the Council," Loup-Garou said from the shadows surrounding the lodge fire. "You're seriously suggesting we raise an army of the dead to send against the soldiers under this colonel's control, and you see nothing evil in that?"

"I see nothing evil in the raising of the dead, sir," Aquinas said quickly. "Their souls aren't being called from the afterlife; only their bodies are being reanimated and sent into battle. It will give you time to evacuate as many of the tribe as possible to the High Prairies and scatter the rest to the winds or another location. The bodies will be used only as distraction. For the most part, getting them to walk will be the extent of what can be done, so the threat of them killing any soldiers is minimal, and no new death energy will be created."

"What's to stop these monsters from simply slaughtering their own troops once this ruse is discovered?" Fights the Wind asked.

Aquinas faced his friend directly. "That's where the second part of this plan comes into play. As long as the completed design is worked into the earth, someone with sufficient power and skill can use it to focus energy and power a massive spell. The actual generation of energy is simple in comparison. We'll have to destroy the pattern as well."

"This pattern is extremely large, and would be impossible to destroy all at once," said a new voice, one with a feminine tone but decidedly edged lilt. The elders turned as one, hands flying to war hatchets and medicine bags as they did. In the shadows nearest the door, the beings Aquinas now knew to be

Iktomi the spider god and Eagle Woman stood quietly, intent gazes focused on the magus who brought this outrageous plan to their people.

"How would you destroy this steel design, magus?" Eagle Woman asked, her gaze like a razor along his face. Aquinas nerved himself to meet her eyes, willing his body not to flinch.

"You're correct. The entire design is too big. However, we've been looking at the problem the wrong way. Since the threat is magical, we've been trying to think of a way to fight it in magical terms. The design is technological in nature, so technology of a different kind might defeat it."

"How?" Eagle Woman asked.

"We don't need to destroy the pattern; we only need to break it. For that, our best bet would be explosives," Aquinas said. His declaration was met with a short laugh from Iktomi and silence from everyone else. The magus took that as a sign to continue.

"If we can break it here," Aquinas gestured to a crude map drawn in the dirt of the lodge floor, "outside Violet Falls, we'll have the best chance of crippling it long-term, perhaps forever. The design crosses the falls here over a long narrow trestle, and according to Lieutenant Caldwell, was the hardest piece of the original plan."

"That's right," the dead man said, for the first time since the meeting started. "The engineers in charge said this span was too wide to be safely bridged, and there is an alternate route that was recommended. However, it would not have closed the circle, which is why Pineville forced the bridge to be built here. Destroy the bridge, and the design is destroyed. The government would never ignore the easier and cheaper route, no matter how much Pineville objects, and he probably won't have the power or time to force the issue."

"Why time?" White Hawk asked.

The dead man shrugged, a jerky motion that made Aquinas shudder. "It's only an impression, but I believe Pineville is on a timetable of some kind. He's spoken of the First, which is the ruler of his realm, in ways that make me think it isn't a patient entity."

The spider god clapped his hands sharply. "Simple enough, then," he said, grin gleaming in the firelight. "Who wants to blow up a bridge with me?"

Calls Thunder Song's brow furrowed, hooding his eyes from the others. "I thought the Spirit Councils were in favor of non-interference in this. Coyote was clear the gods were only interested in withdrawing."

Eagle Woman nodded. "And so they are. Iktomi and I decided Spirit Councils' business was no longer our business, and thus, we may pursue whatever course we choose." She looked at the spider deity for a moment, her eyes amused and sparkling. "My husband, surprisingly, decided he wishes to blow something up, despite the railroads being one of his favorite ideas in all creation. I have something different in mind." Her eyes turned again to the magus, as did almost all others in the lodge save the elder shaman.

Aquinas looked to Calls Thunder Song, seemingly lost in thought and staring into the ineffable flame dancing of the lodge fire. "Any assistance is welcome, but it's not my decision to make. I'm only a diplomatic liaison."

Fights the Wind snorted laughter. The other elders did not share his amusement. White Hawk and Loup-Garou were glowering, while Mangas and the unusually silent Many Voices kept their faces still. "Most diplomats don't lead such exciting lives, Mr. Moore."

Aquinas smiled grimly. "I'm new to diplomacy, I'm

afraid."

At this, Calls Thunder Song smiled, and Aquinas felt a weight lift from his shoulders. The shaman had not given in to despair yet.

"We'll discuss your shortcomings later, Mr. Moore," the old shaman said. "For now, we have much to plan. I'll need your help, magus. Fights the Wind will also stay with us, as will Many Voices; I suspect his skills will be of more use to us."

"You'll have my help as well, shaman," Eagle Woman said sharply. "We may need to battle this colonel's troops directly, and I would not miss that."

"Forgive me, but can you fight without killing? Slaughtering our enemies won't help here," Calls Thunder Song said.

Eagle Woman's eyes narrowed, but her voice was steady. "You'll see how restrained I can be when needed, shaman."

Calls Thunder Song smiled and bowed respectfully. "I mean no insult, Lady of the Blade. Your presence honors and strengthens us." The shaman turned to White Hawk. "Old friend, you and Mangas will take steps to destroy the bridge. It will take stealth and strength in equal measure, so go lightly."

The mighty warrior inclined his head toward the porter, standing by Eagle Woman near the lodge entrance. "With the help of the spider god, a few warriors should be enough."

Calls Thunder Song nodded and turned to Loup-Garou. "You have a harder task, my friend. You must organize our people, get those who can pass through the dreaming ready to depart. Those who cannot must either be evacuated to other places or trained to fight."

The gruff warrior nodded. "I've already begun making plans."

The shaman smiled, having expected as much from his oldest friend. "Then we have our tasks, and little time in which to perform them. I know it's late, but the darkness does not sleep, and neither can we for now."

All of them around the lodge fire, including the dead lieutenant and the deities by the door, nodded in agreement. Time wasn't on their side, and there were many, many obstacles still. Without further words, the elders stood and made their way quickly into the night, leaving Calls Thunder Song, Fights the Wind, Aquinas, Lieutenant Caldwell, Iktomi and Eagle Woman inside the lodge, staring alternately into the cooling flames—now barely more than a scarlet glow about the cinders occasionally flaring into popping orange flickers—and at each other.

"Lieutenant," Fights the Wind finally said, "where can we expect resistance?"

"Yes, dead man," Eagle Woman said. "Show us." She made a sweeping gesture, and the smoke from the lodge fire coalesced into a landscape view, as though they were birds soaring high above the land. None of the elders seemed surprised at this casual display, so Aquinas kept his face still. Little seemed to surprise the lieutenant.

The dead man stared thoughtfully at Eagle Woman's map for a moment before answering. "They'll undoubtedly expect us to fight at the camp site. Unless their powers have grown or changed since I left them, they do not know what we know."

"They surely must know you have come to us," Fights the Wind said.

Caldwell shook his head. "That would be a logical assumption, but they don't think like we do. I believe they'll assume I'm too cowed to defy them in this way, and up until two days ago, they would have been right. They underestimated my revulsion and hatred."

"You were used by them," Aquinas said.

"Magus, how little that phrase covers," Caldwell said bitterly. "Destroyed, driven insane, resurrected with perverse workings powered by lives these hands took; if by that you mean used, then yes." His pale skin gleamed waxy in the fading firelight, and Aquinas stoked the fire, ill at ease with being in the same room as Caldwell with so little light, no matter who else was there. "Understanding their natures, I would stand against them even had I not been their plaything."

"Vengeance can be a useful tool at times," Eagle Woman said. "Perhaps we can make your hatred serve our purpose, Lieutenant."

Calls Thunder Song held up his hand. "Enough of this, my friends. We've started the flood. It's time we figured out how to stay afloat." The shaman faced Aquinas and nodded. "Let's begin with you, Mr. Moore. Tell me how you go about resurrecting an army."

Chapter 16

They shine brighter than the stars, the thing inside Colonel McAlister's skin marveled as it stood outside the command tent, looking over the rows of canvas making up the bivouac of the Tenth Cavalry, United States Army, under its command. Cook fires, lanterns, even the occasional glint of tremulous starlight off the occasional pair of eyes or smiling mouth; all of it shone brilliantly in the augmented spans of McAlister's vision. Better than the glorious shining, though, was the smell, a mobile banquet of warm flesh and vigorous spirit. *These people*, the thing thought, *are stuffed with vitality, brimming with energy they couldn't use in a thousand lifetimes. We need never go hungry here.*

Steps sounded behind it. McAlister recognized the measured tread of the Pineville thing, so continued its sweep of the soldiers camping in the shallow valley below. "Do we have a new toy?"

Pineville sighed. "It appears Lieutenant Caldwell was far more resilient than I gave him credit for. None of the others so far have been able to survive the First's name. I fear we may have to do without for the time being, unless there's enough of Caldwell to reconstitute after the attack is over."

"You think Caldwell was destroyed?" McAlister asked.

"Well, physically anyway," Pineville said. "The magus probably wasn't slowed by the shadow creatures, but stopping Caldwell would require a good deal of physical force; a few fireworks and casual spells wouldn't be enough. I half-expected the magus to die outright."

McAlister sighed and cast its sight around the camp, seeking out another candidate to modify in the same way that Pineville had done for Caldwell. Why Pineville insisted on treating its tools so poorly was a discontent to McAlister. The lieutenant had obviously been of far higher quality than the enlisted men they'd tried to use so far, and yet they were without him again because Pineville wasted him on a trap that wasn't intended to kill the magus. If Pineville wasn't known in the First's realm as a strategic genius, McAlister would never have agreed to work here in this curiously flattened world, regardless of its descendant line's fate or the richness of the local cuisine.

"How go the preparations here?" Pineville asked finally, shaking the colonel gently out of its reverie.

"Troops are ready," McAlister said. "Not many of them seem bothered by the idea of cleaning out an Indian village, though apparently the Shoshone have garnered a reputation as fierce fighters. There are a few, but not as many as I had feared. These cattle are really quite bloodthirsty."

"It's why they taste so good, I think," Pineville said. "Spices the meat wonderfully. I haven't had a chance to sample the young yet, but their females are particularly sweet and tender. You should try some."

"There should be a few in the village," McAlister said. "Are we supposed to take prisoners? I found reference to it in this shell's memories, but he seemed conflicted about it."

"It's considered good form," Pineville said, starting to feel hunger again. The last soldier had been stupid and poorly nourished, not much of a meal. "However, with Indians, nobody will gainsay you if you report they fought to the last soul. Land's easier to settle when it's empty."

McAlister smiled, his mouth grotesquely wide by human standards. In the moonless night, however, there was no human close enough to see. The adjutant staff members who proved themselves useful had been sent off, and the others had been permanently reassigned to dinner. Orders had already been created to explain their absence to the other soldiers, because after all, no sense in spooking the livestock before they had to as far as Pineville and McAlister were concerned.

Pineville looked over the valley filled with tents and equipment, soldiers and support staff, and dreamed of the coming day when the world would be altered to suit its people. It imagined the grandiose temples, turrets and spires of oblong angles stretching into a purple sky in eternal glory to the First and its thousand iridescent offspring. It saw the paths of worship, paved with bones of fallen cattle, lined with the pulsing flesh and muscle of those unworthy of food, kept alive in eternal service as the living veins of the world, surrounding and feeding the First's great flesh, kept potent through digesting souls. Imagining the music of agony, a symphonic shrieking of millions, Pineville smiled at the approach of paradise.

"Are you hungry, McAlister?" Pineville asked, its beloved vision of the future strong in its imagination. Its eye fell on a tent close to the crest of the hill, where an Irish blacksmith's apprentice sullenly patched a leather apron, muttering in pidgin Gaelic about the unfairness of life. *How your life is about to change*, the thing wearing Aldous Pineville's face and skin thought.

McAlister followed the path of Pineville's gaze to the apprentice's tent and smiled appreciatively. Now that the idea was in the air, it could use a late evening meal. Wearing an authoritative expression on the face it had stolen, the thing in McAlister's skin strode purposefully down the hill, a hungry

Pineville hard on its heels. The apprentice was slow and not respectful in the slightest, a common problem among the Irish, or so McAlister's memories said. Nobody would miss him, the things were sure.

Under the starless sky, the camp of soldiers cooked, joked, breathed along with the men who stayed there, all of the Fourth Company, Tenth Cavalry. If anyone heard the muffled sounds of struggle from the tent of a blacksmith apprentice, or heard the wet sounds of creatures taking their feed, they didn't mind or take offense. The darkness, like the soldiers, kept its own counsel in the soft summer evening.

Chapter 17

Constellations like ghosts of distant animals rose and fell with the night; without the moon, it was difficult to tell the time, but as Aquinas stepped out of the shaman's meeting place and stumbled back to his temporary lodge, a glance at the sky told him he was closer to dawn than midnight. Nothing stirred in the night's fading grip, and the magus fervently hoped he could snatch a few short hours of rest before the day came, bringing the promise of death and terrible workings. Although he'd had no time to ponder the possible outcomes of the next 24 hours, he knew he probably wouldn't survive the day.

I've already seen my last sunset, Aquinas thought, and the realization pinched his heart. *I've already drank my last cup of coffee, seen my last play at the theatre.* His mind groped for other events he'd never repeat, but exhaustion forced him on to bed.

The lodge Calls Thunder Song assigned him sat within a large bend in the creek, a brace of yards from what Fights the Wind had identified as one of the better fishing spots. Trout and brookie ran numerous in the reeds and surprisingly deep waters, and if Aquinas had the time, he would have tried his hand at angling there. *Another thing you've already done for the last time*, the dour voice in his head intoned, and Aquinas wearily told his internal doomsayer to be quiet. He trudged down the last steps of the path to his momentary home and walked through the door without even casting a will o'the wisp, clumsily kicking off his boots and doffing his top shirt. Tossing them aside, he half-walked, half-fell into his makeshift bed, and as he put out his hand to grab the soft buffalo hide blanket, he touched a smooth expanse of skin, warm and firm.

Aquinas sputtered a half-formed curse and flung himself backward, sprawling on his back in the dirt. He sat up and heard a rustling from the bedroll as somebody turned in the darkness. *You're in the wrong lodge, idiot*, his internal doomsayer's voice told him, and he stammered an apology as he tried to stand. The fire ring of stones dug painfully into his backside as he gained his footing and stood.

"If finding a woman in your bed is so distressing, magus, you should rethink the direction your life's taken," a familiar voice softly said in the gloom. Aquinas swayed on his feet as he considered the voice. *It couldn't be her*, his doomsayer informed him. He held out his left hand, performed a runesign and narrowed his eyes as a needle of white light blazed in his palm. Magic banished the darkness completely, revealing Eagle Woman in his bedroll, the buffalo hide pulled haphazardly over her lower body. She looked at him expectantly, breasts full and shapely, brown nipples standing out from wood-colored skin in the cool wolf hours.

"I—well, normally I've arranged...er, discussed the situation beforehand," the magus said, carefully looking her in the eyes. It had been some time since he'd seen a naked woman, and he'd never before had a deity in his bed. Besides the potential for mystical trouble, he felt sure Council diplomatic liaisons didn't extend to sex.

"Surprise is one of the spices of life," Eagle Woman said, gracefully standing without apparent effort. The buffalo hide fell away, revealing her body fully. Aquinas couldn't look away, torn between the desire to pull her close and the desire to run like hell. *She's beautiful*, Aquinas thought, *like a well-*

made weapon, an exquisite sword made flesh.

"Eagle Woman," Aquinas began.

She put her finger to his lips. "My husband and I have not known each other in centuries, and it may be centuries before it happens again, even if tomorrow ends well for us. As for now…tomorrow we go into battle, and even deities may die against such magic. You need this, as do I."

Yes, Aquinas thought as she kissed him, the scent of musk and wood smoke mingling in the air. *I do.* He returned the kiss, gently clasping her arms as he did, a tingle of warmth working through his skin and marrow. A flush of heat started from his center and worked outward as blood pounded in his ears and extremities. His limbs trembled as exhaustion dissolved in a roar of adrenaline and desire.

Their first kiss broke, to be replaced by another, more urgent one. His hands began to move down her sleek, muscled frame, pausing at her breasts. A moan escaped her, and powerful hands grabbed at his shirt, then his pants. In a heartbeat, Aquinas stood naked before her, deafened by the thundering of surf in his ears. They tumbled to the bedroll, an electric charge building as energy, drawn by the commingling of magi and animal spirit auras, danced between their bodies. An arc of mystic potential sizzled between them as Aquinas kissed her neck, the hollows of her shoulders, working his way down.

Around them, the air rippled, casting flares of dazzling silver around them as they explored with tongues and hands. Time became liquid; minutes stretched headlong, broke into a heedless run of seasons hot and cold as foreplay gained a deeper rhythm. Eagle Woman took hold of him and guided his body with a sure hand as they settled into each other, rocking slowly in time with the world's heartbeat, moving in the rhythm of the spheres.

Vortices of light spun in Aquinas' vision as his focus narrowed to Eagle Woman's heartbeat, the sweat-slicked curves of her body pressed against his, and the sensation of oneness inside her. They rocked together, taking cues from each other in the joining of human and divine. As the air became close in the lodge, their rhythms accelerated as their breathing became faster, more strained. A sensation of power, sharp and icy, built up in his chest and groin; he felt a similar response building in Eagle Woman, but fiery and jagged in counterpoint. Her breathing was harsh and ragged now, echoing his own gasps.

Long legs flexed and clenched around his waist. Her body opened further to him, pulling him closer inside. Limned in red and purple fire, they glowed like the dimming furnaces of dying suns, and a fleeting part of Aquinas' consciousness wondered if the illumination from his lodge would draw the camp around, pointing and wondering what the hell he was doing. Then Eagle Woman flexed her hips against him, and such wonderings fled. Over their moaning and gasping, Aquinas could hear a sound like waves crashing on eggshells, gaining in strength. It filled his ears as Eagle Woman's body filled his other senses, and his consciousness trembled at the edge of overload.

As he struggled with the urge to give way, he felt a change in Eagle Woman's movement, a sudden tension in her limbs as the peak approached. Marshalling his remaining shreds of control, Aquinas struggled to remember any part of the Tantric disciplines he learned during his Council-sponsored training in India. It was a point of pride that sexual experiences be as pleasurable to his partner as to him, but as they approached climax, Aquinas felt his control falling away in exhaustion and abandon. Finally, as their writhing reached the apex of what they could bear, Aquinas' control disintegrated.

A soundless detonation shook the lodge, kicking up whirlwinds of dust and fibers as mystic fire arced and stuttered across the narrow hut, outlining their bucking forms in flowing lines of power. Cries of passion echoed within the universe bounded by their energy, muscles aching and pounding with released tension as their shared climax made them shudder and quake. Again, moments ran slowly past as passion quieted, and as time resumed its normal pace, exhaustion took Aquinas into sleep, claiming him before he fell to the furs.

Eagle Woman, unable to speak and shaken by the strength of her connection to a mere magus, lay beside Aquinas for a long minute, catching her wind as her heartbeat returned to normal. Her body was jittery and soaked, yet infused with power, as though she could stand up and remake creation before breakfast. She leaned up on one elbow and looked down upon the unconscious magus, gone to the deep sleep of someone too long without it, and smiled. *It would be worth going back to the spider god if the sex were like this,* she thought, and decided against leaving the magus' bed for the night. Iktomi could use a little jealousy, and she could use the sleep.

Thus convinced, Eagle Woman snuggled into the pile of hides and woolen blankets, quickly slipping into slumber. A few stray drops of power sputtered feebly in the darkness and faded as the eastern sky edged into indigo at the sun's still-distant approach. Outside the magus' lodge, a dark figure in a porter's uniform sniffed gently at the air, smiled wistfully, and walked due east to meet the morning head-on.

Chapter 18

Although the things wearing the bodies of Aldous Pineville and Hamish McAlister were not human by even the broadest definition, they did share certain traits and characteristics with mankind, more through thrift of evolutionary tactics than design. Both species had two genders; both were driven by certain primal functions and instincts, more than either might admit. Both species had achieved a certain mastery over their native environments. Both species were afflicted with an overdeveloped sense of curiosity, a trait leading to one species crossing vast gulfs and discovering the other.

Most relevantly, both species dreamed. Frequently, and often uncontrollably, members of both species experienced nighttime fantasies and adventures that were funhouse mirrors of their waking worlds. In the case of the things in the meat suits, their normal existence was already a twisted, depraved reality by human standards, so their dreams…well, often as not, their dreams were of things and places no human would speculate about or understand.

But, occasionally, the things would dream memories, of events that already happened, or omens of great import. Such was the case for the thing now called Pineville, the night before the great design entered the long-planned endgame, as it lay slumped on a cheap military cot in a canvas tent, waiting for dawn to come and slaughter by the hundreds to energize its great Wheel in the earth. Sleep was more of a convention than a necessity, but the cattle required regular sleep, and maintaining cattle habits helped sustain the illusion that Pineville and McAlister belonged among them. So, the thing called Pineville slept, and in sleeping, dreamed.

Free in the dream from Pineville's flesh, it found itself resting in the tallest of the First's temple's pulsing spires, lines of force feeding into it from seven different jagged probes. The First demanded many things from Its followers, among them unfettered access to their minds and several units of miasmic jelly from their fluxioned bodies. Although the First had not seen fit to open Its Eye to Pineville, it felt the withering focus of Its attention, and knew the information would be heard. Folding its primary tentacles into the supplicant stance, it waited for the First to speak.

Aside from the monotonic thrum of the temple's flesh pumps and the hiss of miasmic fluid circulating, silence laid over the supplication space, dense as the spire's membranous shell. Such spires were thought to be of the First's cocooning seed, the remnants of a diaspora predating even the rise and dominion of the tentacled agent's race, who had long since paved over their world's history with the bones of other civilizations. Like many in the First's empire, they had been savage and determined even before the First rewrote their destinies with thaumaturgy and recombinant genetics. For eons, they had been the ruthless arms of the First's will, like scythes to the wheat, and lesser races fell before them.

/report/ came the voice of the First, brass and thunder in Pineville's brain even through the echo of memory. Dreaming, Pineville's tentacles and horns trembled in fear and orgiastic wonder. In the human world, folds like waves on a pond appeared along Pineville's exposed arms as the suit approximated the demands of memory.

"First, a new world has been discovered in our researches," Pineville reported, eyes downcast and tentacles folded in humility. "It has been settled by lesser meat, but it appears it would be easily overwhelmed. They have only the barest knowledge of thaumaturgy, and none at all of technology or Your wonders."

/it should be colonized. my hive swells/ the First said.

"Plans are underway, First. It will require some modification before we can live there unassisted. May I begin the transformation of this world?" Pineville asked its god.

/why waste time with asking/

"In order to live on this world even temporarily as it is now, it is necessary to shed this flesh. I must be reduced to essential miasmic fluid in order to inhabit a host and begin the steps to modify the environment to our needs."

/this flesh is my creation. you repudiate my making?/

"No, First, not for myself. For Your people, for Your presence only. This world and its people are fit for devouring, but our presence cannot be sustained there as it is now. There is a flaw in its fundament that prevents us from surviving there."

From the ordered and analytical spaces of its mind—for all their monstrous natures, the tentacled race were possessed of the keenest intellects in the First's dominion—it willed all of its hard-won technical data, measurements and maps and analyses, to open itself to the First's viewing. For what seemed a trembling eon, the First paged through different sections of Pineville's mind, looking for lies and alternate interpretations, ensuring the agent was telling only truth about what it knew. Threads of gold and white twined into the pipes punched deep into Pineville's body, ready to seize vulnerable places and rend them into quivering agony should the First be disappointed.

At last, the First relinquished its grip on Pineville's mind. The punishing threads withdrew, replaced with replenishing flows of miasmic fluid. The voice of the First sounded again, a tinge of thoughtfulness to its tympanic blare.

/you may proceed. plan well, and take one other. fail not/

A lightning flare of excruciating will blasted into Pineville's body from all seven tubes together. Heat like suns writhing in supernova baked into its flesh as it howled and beat at itself, clawed tentacles pulling in vain at the First's tools. The spire flexed and rumbled in vast amusement, as the First laughed in Pineville's head. The human suit twitched at the memory, bubbling and roiling as its essence attempted to claw loose from the confining meat. Only the thin thread of consciousness remembering what it truly was stopped the dream pain from overwhelming Pineville's panic and shredding its disguise, and safety with it.

/your payment in eternity should you return in failure, supplicant/

"Yes, First. I obey," Pineville gasped in relief as the tubes of miasmic fluid withdrew. Healing pus flowed from the rubbery flesh, sealing the pits over and beginning regeneration. "I shall not fail."

/it is the end of you otherwise. depart/

The spire opened, a veined tubule smoothly ejecting Pineville's massive form back to the vestibule, where it would be scanned and released to the flow of traffic from the holy places into the capital warren of its home planet. As it touched down onto the major artery outside the temple, jagged pain arced through its body from the wounds the First inflicted, and the phantom pain drove Pineville fully awake.

It sat up, disoriented for the briefest of moments, the delicious scent of home still filling its memory even as the human world crowded into its awareness. The limitations of two eyes struck home, and Pineville was again a miasmic fluid creature in a biped shell of meat and bone, not the glorious offspring of a singular intelligence vaster than galaxies. It sighed at being trapped in limited, decaying matter yet again, and decided it had enough of blending in with the cattle for one night.

Pineville, fully awake, opened the flap of the colonel's command tent and looked out over the encampment below. Outside the tent, the colonel stood, smoking a cigar and watching the stars sail against the black velvet of space. Humans could not perceive anything beyond the shimmer of visible light through the suffocating atmosphere, but even limited by stolen flesh, the things saw a wondrous spectrum of radiation and energy, even wavelengths human physics would never discover. The sweet smell of tobacco, mingled with the sweeter smell of burned flesh, reached Pineville's nose, and its mouth began to water.

"Haven't mastered cigars yet," the thing wearing McAlister said as Pineville came to stand beside it. It held a hand up against the moon to illustrate. Pineville saw blisters forming on the first two fingers, suppurating in the silvery coolness. While moving about in the flesh disguises was now easy enough, the perception of damage still wasn't working correctly. Very little in this world could cause them true pain, and as a result, Pineville forced himself to be careful in avoiding excessive damage to his suit. McAlister hadn't internalized that lesson yet.

"After tomorrow, it won't matter," Pineville said. "Just keep your riding gloves on until the change, and then, we can finally escape these suits. I look forward to my own body again."

McAlister nodded and took another long puff from the cigar. Smoke dribbled from its nose and mouth. "Dreamed of home?"

"Yes," Pineville said, "the day the First allowed me to leave and come here."

"Such honor," McAlister said. "Your line will feed at the foot of the First's shadow for millennia once this world is opened."

"How were you chosen?" Pineville asked. "Did you plead before the First?"

McAlister barked laughter. "I've never had the privilege of facing the First. No, my line was judged guilty of some heresy--I don't know which one--and I was allowed the opportunity to redeem my line's existence by coming here." McAlister idly peeled damaged skin from its fingers as it spoke, dropping the shreds to the ground. Blood and pus dripped freely down its arm.

"You must have immense value to the First, then."

The colonel shrugged. "I think my forebears' torment is unusually sweet to the Eye. It is irrelevant. All I care about is I've been granted a chance to redeem whatever error was made." McAlister tossed the cigar aside and wiped its bloody hands on the uniform pants it wore. "The fact the cattle are so fine here is agreeable."

"Wait until the plan is complete," Pineville said. "I promise you a feast."

The things stood together on the hill, looking over the valley as the men below slept or talked quietly, unaware of their oncoming deaths and the end of everything they knew. Above them, uncaring stars twinkled in the black, keeping their spectrums and secrets from human eyes.

Chapter 19

Hot and sharp the dawn rose, the promise of fire already on the wind as Iktomi strode toward the small group of men waiting by the wide creek that anchored the camp. Even if the spider god hadn't known the Shoshones and their leaders, he would have known White Hawk and Mangas as elders of the tribe. Their tanned and lined faces marked them as old, but the power and pride inherent in their stance, how they addressed the younger men, the confidence with which they moved; these traits marked them in Iktomi's eyes as leaders, pillars of strength. The trickster spirit knew he had the right men for the task.

"Spider god," White Hawk said as Iktomi reached them, his newly cleaned porter's uniform incongruous in the new day, "can you move us where we need to go? Violet Falls is nearly a day's ride away."

"Not directly; the design is too deep an energy well for that," Iktomi said, "but we can step through the dreaming to a point close by. We should hurry. The gathering power makes the dreaming harder to cross by the second, and if the Spirit Councils act before us, we may find ourselves too far away or trapped between spaces."

"Then why wait?" White Hawk said.

Iktomi nodded and spread his hands as if releasing a bird. Before him, a patch of air roughly the size of a door shimmered and rippled, finally parting to reveal an arched portal into an obsidian world. *The darkness is overpowering the spaces between*, Iktomi thought as he looked deep into the darkness, parsing the paths to every possible point, discarding universes and timelines like a seamstress might discard swatches of cloth.

"We're walking into that?" one of the younger men asked.

"Unless you prefer fleeing," Mangas said in an authoritative tone. The younger men subsided and waited for the elders to command them, only their restless eyes giving any sign of unease. Iktomi approved of their discipline. "Ah, history," the spider god said to himself as he found the half-felt, half-seen distortion in the dreaming, sensing the warping of the meridians and ley lines around steel laid over the earth.

"There's the design," Iktomi said, "and…there, the path to our destination." A shaft of sunlight seemed to stretch from the physical world along a wall of ebon emptiness, a road of light wound over and through invisible deformations in the dreaming. Slivers of turbulence danced around the path, causing wakes in the air above and around it, but the path itself was solid and unyielding. Iktomi's godhood was still as potent in the dreaming as in the physical world, he was relieved to see.

"Red Wolf, do you have the dynamite?" Mangas asked. The tallest of the young men, a brave built like an oak with a jagged scar across his chest, held up a satchel and nodded. A war hatchet was slung from one hip, a large Bowie knife from the other. Two bandoliers of ammunition crossed his broad torso, and a rifle was hung from one mighty shoulder. All the Shoshone were similarly attired but for White Hawk, who carried nothing but a matched pair of hatchets.

"Where are your other weapons?" Iktomi asked White Hawk as he approached.

"With the enemies I haven't killed yet," the elder answered. Iktomi smiled. He liked White Hawk's general attitude.

"Mangas, you and Red Wolf will head for the bridge as soon as we reach Violet Falls," White Hawk said. "The rest of the men and I will form a guard. If need be, we'll create a distraction. Spider god, can you disguise our actions from magical viewing?"

Iktomi shrugged. "Somewhat, but my very presence will cause a disturbance. I can withdraw within the dreaming and hide myself from this world, but I don't know how long I can stay there. "

White Hawk and Mangas looked at each other, holding a wordless conversation in moments. Iktomi envied humans the ability to form friendships like that. Gods were not noted for their interpersonal skills.

It was Mangas who broke the momentary silence. "No, spider god. Having you at the ready with us is worth the risk. We'll have to be swift." He gestured to the braves. "Follow us, and be ready."

Like the elders of the Shoshone people they were, White Hawk and Mangas entered first, running at a quick pace for men their age. Red Wolf and the other braves followed, easily keeping pace as they kept their weapons ready. Iktomi followed closely behind. As he entered the portal, he cast a complex marking rune that pinned the portal's location to the camp. Even if forced to close the portal at the other end and sever the connection, the spider god could open another portal and home in on the anchored rune to create another path. Whether the dreaming would be traversable was a different question.

"Keep to the path," Iktomi called as he ran, following the braves. He clearly saw the disorientation of the corrupted dreaming set in as the mission party stumbled and wove across the path. Through the distortion, the spider god could see White Hawk and Mangas reach the portal—a door-shaped

patch of sunlight and blue sky—and call back to the braves.
Almost to the door, Red Wolf stumbled the last few feet and
sprawled in the dirt outside. The darkness had almost completely consumed the dreaming, even clouding Iktomi's senses.
He realized his die was cast. Not only would he have to stay
in the human world as Mangas and White Hawk led their men,
but they needed another way home, magical or not, if the darkness could not be expelled.

Of course, he told himself, *if the plan doesn't work, getting home won't be a concern anyway.*

The second brave, the youngest of the warriors, followed
closely on Red Wolf's heels and made it through the portal, but
Iktomi saw the other braves were not as fortunate. He ran to
catch up as the middle brave, a young man whose name Iktomi
hadn't learned, stumbled and fell to his knees. Before Iktomi
could shout a warning, the brave fell, clutching his stomach
and rolling off the edge of the path entirely. A liquid sound,
like the warping of metal, tore through the air as the brave fell
into the darkness, and an agonized scream echoed through the
dreaming as the brave was shredded by rippling waves of reality, his body disintegrated into millions of howling particles.
At the other end, White Hawk roared something unintelligible,
his voice coarsened and slowed into a parody of his bass growl.

The brave closest to Iktomi was on the verge of falling
when the spider god caught him, grabbing him by the bandoliers and slinging him over his shoulder with a god's strength.
Without breaking stride, Iktomi increased his speed over the
bends and furrows of the light path, twisting and folding as
the darkness tried to shatter the illuminated road. He leaped
into space, eyes locked with divine focus, and sailed over
weakened architectures of light, twisted into constructions
of geometries humans wouldn't have the math to describe

for decades, if ever. The spider god landed nimbly on a linear section, scooped up the last surviving brave, hanging onto the path edge with grim determination, and launched himself into the sunlight.

White Hawk and Mangas dove aside as Iktomi and his passengers re-emerged, shoulder-rolling to either side of the portal and leaping to their feet before the trickster spirit could touch ground. Even burdened with two disoriented men, the spider god was as nimble as his arachnid children. As the warriors watched, Iktomi neatly flipped in the air, twisted his body, and came down lightly on his feet, facing the party with a brave under each powerful arm. The darkness, hungry and sensing the loss of something valuable, pushed and bulged against the portal, but the spider god's will, glowing in his perceptions like sunlight, kept the darkness penned neatly within the dreaming. With a snap of intention, Iktomi closed the portal regretfully, sealing the angry darkness within.

"Our way home is no more," Iktomi told the party as he gently put the men down, allowing them to catch their breaths as the disorientation faded. "Darkness consumes the dreaming, and I cannot pass us through it again. Perhaps Coyote can still do so."

"No matter," White Hawk said. "If our task isn't done, it is irrelevant, and if it's completed, we may have the option again. Let's say a brief prayer for our fallen comrade and be off."

Time is fading, Iktomi thought, but one look at White Hawk's face told him this needed to be done. Even spider gods don't need angry tribal leaders at their back. Iktomi came to believe over the centuries the time of gods was long past due to end, and it was likely times and men like these that put the final nails in the gods' coffins, so to speak. Without gods, there

could be no darkness of this magnitude. Of course, Iktomi reflected, that didn't mean he was ready yet for the long twilight.

The men said a brief prayer so their comrade, a brave
with the name of Wind Dancer, would find his way to the High
Prairies and be welcomed there by his ancestors. Iktomi sent
a message to Coyote through the worlds, but he couldn't tell
if it went or if Coyote had received it. The darkness likely
swallowed it, the same way it swallowed Wind Dancer, and
smashed it into oblivion. Iktomi held his anger in check; there
would be time for that later, or there wouldn't. Either way, he
had other tasks.

White Hawk looked around to take their bearings. The
portal deposited them roughly half a mile from town and nearly a mile south of the bridge. Luck was with them so far, as the
party was atop a short hill giving them an excellent view of
the heat-seared plain and the river canyon the bridge spanned.
After a whispered conference with White Hawk, Mangas and
Red Wolf began moving toward the bridge, covering ground
quickly without obviously running. They kept low, and vanished into the trees and brush wedged between Violet Falls and
the steel bridge.

"Spider god," White Hawk said, "what can you tell us
about the town right now?"

The other men looked at each other quizzically, but Iktomi understood White Hawk's meaning. The wise elder suspected some force was arrayed against them here, and wanted
to know if Iktomi could detect it before an alarm went up. He
opened his perceptions wide and read the town below them
carefully, brushing over every mind and emotional state in
town with a gossamer touch, leaving no disturbance or sign
of his presence.

"No alarm yet," Iktomi said, "no sense of caution or concern. However, I cannot read telegraph messages on the line, so if something comes through that way, I won't know it until the word gets out."

"We'll need a backup plan," White Hawk said. "I know you can read men's thoughts, but can you send a thought to one person?"

"Yes," Iktomi said.

"Good. Send a thought to Mangas and let him know Crowkiller and I will follow them at a distance. If we're caught, we'll raise a distraction so they can continue. If they're caught, we'll continue on. Cloud Watcher will stay here and watch over you, spider god."

Iktomi raised an eyebrow at White Hawk's authoritative tone. The elder quickly added, "Please."

The spider god nodded. "Done. I'll send you a thought if anything changes."

White Hawk nodded in return, and the war leader and Crowkiller quickly headed off in a parallel direction to the first party. Having nothing better to do but wait, Iktomi sat cross-legged on the ground, and kept a careful watch over the town of Violet Falls, hoping his intervention wouldn't be needed.

A brilliant flare of emotional energy shot into Iktomi's sight less than five minutes later, ruining his hope for a quick and easy operation. A cry of alarm echoed in his head, immediately followed by the sharp report of a Winchester rifle. *.30/06 from the sound*, Iktomi thought. Technology and its tools were his purview, after all...He shook his head and focused on the men below. Mangas and Red Wolf were still unspotted, making their way down a curved and narrow path cut into the canyon side, but Crowkiller had been spotted by someone carrying a rifle—a rancher, perhaps—and had been shot at. Neither Crowkiller nor White Hawk were injured, but the shot drew attention, and Iktomi sensed by the racing plans and suppressed thrill in White Hawk's mind the elder planned to capitalize on it.

Iktomi scanned the area for obstacles and people. *Turn left at the alley behind the livery, White Hawk, and you can escape into the trees. No houses back there.*

White Hawk's reply, cool and deep like his speaking voice, arrowed back to Iktomi at once. *Not ready to escape yet. We need to draw more people over here.*

Iktomi smiled. *Then turn right; you're two buildings down from what looks like a brothel.*

Laughter, so loud Iktomi thought he heard it in the air, echoed in his mind as White Hawk agreed. Fleeting expressions of exertion and confusion bubbled over the town, to be replaced by great yellow gouts of panic and terror as a brothel's worth of working girls saw two armed Shoshones break in through the back, faces wearing terrifying grimaces to hide their mirth. Now, Iktomi was sure he could hear the noise from town, screams and wood splintering as the warriors kicked over tables and shattered doors. Cloud Watcher stirred next to him, but did not pause in watching the immediate area for threats.

Iktomi sensed an impromptu posse forming, and passed the location (*three buildings down, other side of the street*) along to White Hawk. With another piece of his attention, he sought out Mangas, who had reached the canyon floor with Red Wolf and was fording the wide creek.

We're there now, the elder thought in bright red and white tones, splashing Iktomi's vision with a vitality barely hinted at in his demeanor. *Running low on time?*

White Hawk and Crowkiller are having fun. How close are you?

A pause, then a bloom of concern, green and spreading under Mangas' practiced calm. *We're planting the explosives, but we underestimated how much we would need. The trestle supports are much thicker and more numerous than expected. I don't think we have enough.*

The spider god cursed in a long-forgotten tongue, did it again as another shot rang out, and an orange-blue flare of pain spouted into view. A quick scan confirmed Crowkiller had been shot in the arm. The wound was merely scoring and wasn't serious, but it would slow them down and make it tougher to evade the posse, gathering steam now as the Shoshone slowed in their flight. Cloud Watcher briefly looked over the town, seeing more in Iktomi's face than from Violet Falls. The brave said nothing, but the concern radiating from his aura was plain to see.

Spider god, called White Hawk, *how close are Mangas and Red Wolf? We're running out of room.*

There are many sources of trickery and wisdom in the far-flung pantheon of gods, but few as clever or as mischievous as Iktomi, especially under pressure. His powers may not be as world-shaking or powerful as his brother Coyote or Raven, or his spiritual twin Anansi, but they have rarely been insufficient. As he cast about for an answer to give to the valiant elder who Iktomi respected almost above any humans save the father and son shamans of the tribe, mischief danced brightly in his mind and presented an idea to his human façade, a plan wrapped in red, yellow and white bows just begging to be opened. And, best of all, he saw how he could accomplish his goal without doing much, appealing to the fundamental laziness of all tricksters.

New plan, White Hawk, Iktomi sent to the elder. *Can you get back to the livery with Crowkiller?*

Not without being seen, White Hawk replied.

Don't worry about that. Cloud Watcher is on his way; when he comes barreling into town, make your escape. Iktomi ignored the protest already forming in White Hawk's thoughts and gave Cloud Watcher the order to steal a horse, ride through town at a fast gallop, shoot out as many windows as he could without getting shot, lose any and all pursuit, abandon the horse, and make his way back to their vantage point without being seen.

Cloud Watcher said nothing for a few seconds, then asked, "Is that all?"

Iktomi nodded. Cloud Watcher shrugged, ran down the hill, and vanished into the trees, invisible even to Iktomi's perceptions. *Impressive*, thought Iktomi, and turned his attentions to Mangas. Warned by the shots, they planted the explosives and hid themselves in the thick bushes against the base of the canyon wall.

Mangas, Iktomi sent, *you and Red Wolf get up here and keep hidden until I tell you to move. Steal a couple of horses and make your way back to the vantage point.*

What? The bridge isn't destroyed yet, Mangas replied. *I'm not here to steal horses, spider god.*

Plans change, Iktomi said. *Got a plan that doesn't require explosives.*

Are you confident in that? Mangas asked.

I'm a god, Iktomi replied. *I'm always confident.*

I'm a human, Mangas thought, *and we know shit happens. I'll finish planting these and set the fuse.*

Iktomi laughed. *Fair enough. How fast can you climb?*

Just finished; we're on the way. Hope those nags I saw in the orchard are faster than they look.

Iktomi smiled again and got to his feet slowly. He had

been careful so far, using only the most passive of his powers on the off chance agents of the darkness were in the area and on the lookout for mystic endeavors. He wasn't worried for himself—tricksters rarely are—but he was convinced the white magus and the ancient shaman were right about necromantic magic arrayed against them, and that wild magic could overwhelm even the gods. The plan risked enough as it was.

Still, there was a time for caution, and that time was done. To take down the Violet Falls bridge, and the great steel design with it, required a bold stroke. The time for camouflage was over. Iktomi the spider god, lord of mischief and technology, master of webs and potions, focused on the midpoint of the bridge and pulled himself right out of the world. In a blink, he put himself on the bridge, traversing more than a mile in less time than it took to see it. When he arrived, his body was no longer that of a Negro porter in an immaculate uniform, but that of a red and yellow striped spider, six feet across with white lightning jags on his abdomen, his eight eyes sparkling with mirth and purpose. Around the town, Iktomi felt the subtle springs of warnings, the unheard clicking of traps being triggered, and he knew great jags of obscene force were probably on their way toward his vulnerable body, his truest form.

He chattered a bemused expletive in the spider tongue, mandibles clicking, and a great joy coursed through him. With a thought, his spinneret spat a thick glob of spider silk onto the steel rails, and he leaped off the bridge, using a slender cable of silk to draw him short and swing him into the bridge's latticed understructure. Eight legs skated across wood and iron, and within moments, a circular web had formed among the support struts, blinding white against the dull gray and brown of the mighty trestle. *I have maybe a minute left*, Iktomi thought, *before hell breaks loose against me. Surely enough time for one more round.*

The great spider wove even faster, and a grander pattern emerged from the webbing, a mandala against evil, containing the many runes Iktomi used in years past in various mischiefs and good deeds. His perceptions remained clear, and he sensed the power arrayed against him was awesome in scope. Some of it would be deflected by the steel, but not nearly enough, and the possibility of a mortal wound was very real. However, it wasn't enough to take down the bridge, and he suspected that was intentional. *Perhaps the darkness expected this tack*, he thought bemusedly.

Iktomi, what in Coyote's name are you doing? Don't you see what's coming? White Hawk thought.

He's getting good at this, Iktomi thought. *He even used my name.*

Get your people to safety, elder, Iktomi replied. *I'm honored to have known you, and look forward to meeting you again.*

What--, came the reply, but the spider god cut him off. He already sensed that White Hawk and Crowkiller had made their escape. Mangas and Red Wolf were making their way undiscovered back to the hill with a trio of mustangs, and Cloud Watcher rode a stolen pony from a farm into the nearby tree line even as he turned his sight on him. The Shoshones would disappear into the land, and if they were truly fortunate, would find a people waiting for them when they returned.

And now, the spider thought as he completed his web and leaped nimbly to the top of the bridge, *the last and best part.* Leaning over the edge, the great spider stared into the deep canyon below and opened up a portal directly beneath the trestle. A door-sized patch of nothing appeared in the creek, and the hungry darkness, primed for the taste of trickster, flowed from the portal. Tentacles, thick and evil-veined, shot into the light, homing inerrantly on the prey it sought: the sweet scent of spider, the delicious tang of immortal god, now strung in sticky loops and lines all over the bridge superstructure.

"Bon appétit," the spider god roared with laughter, squeezing his godhead into the human form he enjoyed so well, and which gave off the least sign of his power. He leaped to his feet as the darkness looped around metal beams emblazoned with strands of silk and heaved, inexorably pulling them into the maw of the portal now kept in check only by Iktomi's will. As the web fractured under the darkness' pull, the bridge began to warp and splinter. Steel rails bent and groaned under the pressure. Beams of oak splintered and burst. Sparks and splinters filled the air, and the bridge rippled like waves. Along the rails, Iktomi ran, laughter bubbling from him even as human breathing grew harsh in his chest. The tortured steel began to screech, and the center of the bridge sagged, cracking ties and joined beams asunder.

Iktomi was still thirty feet from the canyon lip when a string of detonations roared up from the base of the trestle, showering the canyon floor with dirt and debris from the damaged, but not destroyed, supports, filling Iktomi's ears with glorious roars. Although Mangas had been right about not having enough dynamite, with the supports damaged, the bridge slewed to the west, snapping the rails apart. His balance shifted beneath him, and from his perspective, the world began to slew to his right even as he ran, appearing as if he was sliding in place.

A shame the dynamite won't affect the darkness, Iktomi thought; it had no physical form to affect, only force and intention, neither of which mere explosives could touch. He stumbled and fell to one knee. The slewing increased, and Iktomi grabbed a railroad tie as the bridge became a falling ladder, the fall picking up speed as the darkness swallowed more of the bait Iktomi had laid out. Climbing was out of the question for now. His human form couldn't adjust to the falling fast enough, and turning back into a spider would simply draw the darkness, still searching for trickster meat.

Twisting, the ladder on which Iktomi clung sped toward the jagged stone of the canyon wall, a pendulum approaching a clock wall that wouldn't yield. The spider god who looked like a porter spared a moment to look down at what he had wrought. Although still questing here and there, the immolating sunlight had kept most of the tentacles from reaching into the day for more than a handful of seconds. However, between the explosions and the hungry void, that had been enough to utterly destroy the bridge. Shattered and twisted beams littered the canyon floor, and only one of the original supports still stood. Sawdust and the scent of heated metal filled the air, and only a few tentacles were still reaching from the portal, hugging the scant shadows on the canyon floor. Still, that was a few too many.

"That's enough," the spider god said aloud, and closed the portal. Subdued by the mid-morning sun, the darkness was unable to fight back, and the portal closed easily, shutting in the darkness with its empty meal. The space where it had been remained for a moment, but was quickly erased by the creek's muddy flow. In a heartbeat, only the froth and bubble of water remained.

Good, he thought. Then the world was impact and dust, the clanging of stressed steel and ruptured wood against rock, and the spider god fell, pulled into gravity's greedy embrace. The spider god twisted in the air, feeling his mortal body accelerate toward the rocky floor, and laughed at the sensation.

Falling is wonderful, he thought joyfully. *I should really try it again sometime.*

Iktomi watched the ground get closer, and he understood stopping would not be nearly the joy falling was. *However*, he thought, *I am the wise and mischievous spider god. I'm sure I'll think of something.* Impatiently, he waited to see what his next idea was.

Chapter 20

Morning met the soldiers of the Tenth Cavalry already in motion, a column of men and equipment snaking across the prairie, eyes watchful and weapons ready. Had McAlister ordered a guerrilla skirmish, using tactics so frequently turned against large armies by smaller forces, the men would have rode forth in the dead of night, but the things inside the meat suits of Pineville and McAlister wanted large-scale slaughter to power their design. The Shoshone didn't know it was coming to them, so there would be no shortage of victims to use.

Near the middle of the column, McAlister and Pineville rode together, each astride large nervous bays, skittish from their dim sensing of the things inside the bodies. Both were at relative peace, seeing a plan long in motion come to completion and looking forward to the meal ahead, their first real taste of the paradise to come. The soldiers moved briskly but without hurry, settling into the pace of men used to traveling long distances with nothing to do but gaze at the scenery and wait.

While McAlister discussed plans and logistical matters with its underlings, none of whom were aware of the colonel's true nature, Pineville sat quietly. It had been reviewing the plan over and over in its mind all morning, ticking off the points and pieces in order, looking for weak spots and areas of attack. Something was arrayed against the plan, something with an incomplete knowledge of its true design but the ability to keep out of the things' perceptions, at least until this moment. Through rumor and investigation, Pineville had narrowed the likely suspects to the father and son shamans of the Shoshone tribe, although that was no great feat. Calls Thunder Song and Fights the Wind were the only local talents capable of covering their tracks so well, so lack of finding anyone else probably pointed right to them. Still, Pineville did not know, and worse, did not know how much they might know. That was another reason why the Shoshone were chosen as the sacrifice to bring this world into alignment with the First: while he wasn't concerned about their mystic skills, it seemed prudent to remove any threat they might represent.

"The cattle make good time," McAlister said sotto voce to Pineville, their horses next to each other. Pineville noted McAlister handled its horse with far greater ease and authority, despite its lack of experience in this world. The observation irritated Pineville.

"Let's hope they kill with as much expediency," Pineville snapped. A worm of unease crawled along its back, all the more disturbing because it could not pinpoint the cause. Except for Lieutenant Caldwell's disappearance, every step had gone smoothly: the soldiers were on the move, the focus wheel of steel and distance was complete and charged, miasmic reality had infiltrated the cross-spaces of this world. Everything was as it predicted, exactly as it needed to be in order to begin the spell and prepare the way for the First.

"You're not a very good winner," McAlister noted, smiling. Pineville did not appreciate McAlister's humor, nor its ease in employing it. It was clear that McAlister was far better adapted to this world than Pineville, despite having many months of experience more than the newcomer, and it resented this. *Didn't I give up far more of my life, risking the First's wrath for this project?* Pineville thought. *This is my work, my glory in the First's name.*

"Things are still in motion," Pineville said darkly. It didn't believe the plan was threatened...but McAlister believing in a threat wasn't all bad, Pineville thought. There was that nagging feeling, too, something Pineville couldn't uncover and couldn't explain away.

"The lieutenant is of no consequence," McAlister said. Pineville started in its seat; did McAlister have the same thoughts, or was McAlister invading its mind? "The Shoshone won't believe anything an Army officer has to say, much less one obviously dead, even if Caldwell wasn't turned into paste by the shaman. You worry too much."

"You don't face the First's wrath if we fail," Pineville said quietly.

"Whatever wrath you face doesn't outweigh my line's extinction," McAlister replied in the same soft tone. "I am concerned for them, but the project will succeed. I've staked my life on it, same as you."

Pineville fell silent, angered by McAlister's boldness and unsure of how to answer. It had indeed staked its life on the worldmaking, but admittedly, extinction of an entire line did carry more weight. Even Pineville's concern for its existence, however, didn't match the unease it felt. Something more was needed.

The sound of galloping reached Pineville, and it shook itself from its reverie as a gangly scout thundered up to their position and dismounted in a flash. Snapping off a hasty salute, the scout told the colonel there was something up ahead needing McAlister's attention.

"What is it, Private?" McAlister snapped, letting the brogue the colonel used when angry slip into his voice.

"It's...well, sir, I don't know what it is. It could be an army, but I've never heard or smelled one like it."

"Smelled, soldier?" McAlister said. The scout nodded, and Pineville saw that underneath the flush of exertion and travel dirt, the young scout was pale as milk. He swallowed several times as McAlister glared at him, as if trying to keep his last meal in his stomach.

"There's a lot of them, sir, and they smell real bad. Like death."

McAlister frowned, but spurred his mount forward. "Show me."

"Yes, sir." The scout clambered back on his horse, wheeled it around expertly, and galloped off in the opposite direction, McAlister close behind. Although Pineville had no rank on this journey, he dug into his mount's flanks and was soon alongside the colonel. Within a minute, they were at the front of the column, which had ridden up to the crest of a low rise that tumbled down a weak slope into a broad valley below. Pineville caught up to the colonel and looked down into the valley, his nose already registering notes of decay, turned earth, and grave moss before he could see what awaited them.

Spread across the valley was an army of motionless forms, standing with inhuman patience, awaiting the march of the Tenth. Many of the forms gazing up at them were dressed in Shoshone raiments in various stages of rot, but Pineville saw a few dressed as Lakota, a handful of Apache, and a scattering of other tribes. There were even a few white men and Mexicans, as well as a clutch of Chinese laborers, coolie hats of discolored and rotted straw speckling their faces with shade. Even if the smell had not given it away, Pineville recognized them by their sterile and colorless auras: the resurrected dead, brought to a half-life and given motion by a strong and complex spell working. Hundreds strong, the army of the dead stood silently waiting for the living to advance. The unease in Pineville's thoughts changed to disquiet when it saw the crisply uniformed man standing at the front of the army, his pale face unmarred save for a deep furrow across one cheek.

"He couldn't have raised this army," McAlister said, its voice thoughtful.

"No, but he appears to be leading it," Pineville replied in a tight voice. Deep rage boiled through Pineville, so strong its breath was shortened, its head light and ringing in the aftermath. Unbidden, the spell Pineville used to resurrect Caldwell leapt to mind, its complexities unrolling as an enraged miasmic being looked for a way to undo its working, preferably with the maximum of suffering.

Caldwell walked toward the mounted things, his hands raised in a gesture of welcome. His gait was natural and smooth, but the soldiers in the front of the column were visibly spooked at his approach, muttering amongst themselves and furtively making religious gestures. Caldwell had been well-known to the Tenth Cavalry, as were the stories of his rampage aboard the Santa Fe Pacific Express and his subsequent death. As he approached, and the deep wound on his face became clearer, the heady scent of fear wafted through the ranks, and the horses began to stir and pull away. Caldwell grinned wider, exposing his teeth through the cheek.

"Stand your ground, men," McAlister shouted in a clear voice. "There's nothing to fear from this poor bastard."

Caldwell stopped his approach a handful of yards away and sketched a casual salute in McAlister's direction. "Lieutenant Anderson Caldwell, late, of the U.S. Army, reporting for duty with new allies." Caldwell turned to gesture at a knot of Shoshone medicine women nearby, nervously standing their ground and conspicuously unarmed. "Here to stop your world-making project, Colonel." Caldwell nodded toward Pineville, who felt a snarl rising in its throat at Caldwell's cocky smile. "Mr. Pineville, what a pleasant surprise to see you again."

"Lieutenant, if you weren't dead, you'd be hanging from the gallows right now," McAlister said gruffly. "I don't know what a hanging would do to you, but I'd be willing to find out. Perhaps you'd make do with a firing squad? There don't seem to be many trees out here."

"Colonel, that's a tempting proposition, but I must respectfully decline," Caldwell replied. "I have a duty to perform first."

"Lieutenant...no, Mr. Caldwell," McAlister said, "whatever this little fantasy is you've concocted, best submit to military custody right now. Not only are you a murderer several times over, but you're interfering in lawful maneuvers of the United States Army."

"That's an interesting interpretation, Colonel," Caldwell said, smiling broadly in the morning sunshine. "We both know you're not here on business of the United States. You're here for...what was his name again?"

The dead man thought for a moment, then looked at Pineville and uttered a long series of thorned and twisted syllables, harsh and liquid, like a tumbler of lye. No human palate could make the sounds Caldwell had heard, but he did his best to repeat them, knowing humans would be unaffected by his attempt. However, he suspected the things in the meat suits would not be, and he was proved correct; at his words, both McAlister and Pineville screeched, inhumanly high like dying raptors, and fell off their mounts, clutching at their ears in vain to block the blasphemy of Caldwell's voice.

"Its Name, polluted!" howled McAlister, rolling with pain in the hardpan dust. Thin clouds of dirt rose around the colonel as it caterwauled.

Pineville roared, teeth gnashing as it held its head in both hands. Blood and spittle flew from its mouth as it howled, cursing Caldwell in its native tongue. Shreds of skin peeled from its throat as the human shell tried in vain to reproduce the words, calling on the First to halt the dead man's offense against Its glory. Soon Pineville's mouth was a frothing slash of red in a pale face as Caldwell continued his mocking attempts to say the First's name.

Dimly, both miasmic beings heard the panicked neighing of the horses as cavalrymen tried to calm their horrified mounts, but neither thing cared. Only the agony pouring into their ears, burning into their cores, mattered. Finally, mercifully, Caldwell stopped, laughing with glee as the things rolled and coughed in the dust and blood-soaked mud their bodies churned up. Over the stench of his own blood and scorched skin, Pineville smelled the panic in the ranks, full-bodied as the word spread of the confrontation between the dead man and the colonel.

"And that's just the first of it," Caldwell said, brushing dust from his uniform casually while he waited for the colonel and Pineville to regain their composure. The things in the human shells gained their feet and stood before Caldwell, sheer rage keeping them standing even as discipline failed those behind them. Pineville took a step toward the lieutenant, its heart set on ripping the feeble soul from Caldwell's animated corpse and shredding it before swallowing every sliver. It even knew the exact spell it wanted to use, every eldritch rune and syllable waiting to leap from Pineville's mind into the world.

Caldwell smiled again, with a far darker edge this time. "You had your chance, creature." With far more speed than Pineville expected of him, Caldwell lunged forward and delivered a powerful left cross to Pineville's throat. Pineville felt the cartilage crunch and skin bruise under Caldwell's knuckles, and the impact sent it flying backward to land in a boneless heap, several feet in front of its mount. Already frightened by what was inside the shell, the skittish bay reared, braying with panic and narrowly missing Pineville's skull with its stamping hooves. It reared again and bolted before the stunned Pineville could move.

McAlister began to shout an order to its men, but before it could verbalize the command, reality shifted under Pineville's perception. Daylight grew more intense, the power lines running through the earth and the air above it blazed brighter in its perceptions, and a sense of immense pressure, like mountains of water behind a dam shifting, pressed upon Pineville's skin. Horror took hold of Pineville, and as it sat up, seeing the same look on McAlister's face, it didn't notice the boneless shifting of its head on a broken neck, the lolling to the right as the head tried to rest on splintered vertebrae and failed. The soldiers didn't notice the shift in the ley lines around them, but they did see Pineville's body continue to move after a fatal injury, and combined with the army of the dead before them, the unspoken command to run flashed among the soldiers like signal down a telegraph line.

"I believe there's a bridge that needs rebuilding," Caldwell said aloud, his hands raised to heaven in hallelujah. Pineville and McAlister reached out their perceptions as one, and saw the great focus wheel they designed and built from railroad steel and human sweat was now broken, one segment completely erased. All the energy marshaled, all the intention and spell work laid down with great time and effort in preparation for the immense bloodletting to remake the world: gone. A terror greater than any abyss squeezed Pineville's mind.

With a casual wave of his hand, Caldwell motioned

the army of the dead forward. "Attack," he said simply, and moved forward on the things in the human suits, drawing his saber with an unmistakable look of glee.

Chapter 21

Far behind the army of the dead, a tribal circle, sketched into the dry brown prairie floor and surrounded by runes, hummed with power. Within the circle, three men sat facing each other, eyes open but unseeing as each looked inward to work their magic. Aquinas sat facing north, quietly chanting the overarching couplets of the resurrection spell over and over. Fights the Wind and Calls Thunder Song, facing east and west respectively, chanted a Shoshone elemental refrain in counterpoint to simultaneously call up all the dead bodies in a mile-wide radius and convince them that no dishonor was meant in summoning them from their graves. Aquinas had his doubts about the second part of the spell, but as resurrection spells were occasionally known to dredge up hostile spirits, it seemed a fair precaution.

Outside the circle, Eagle Woman kept a close watch on the proceedings, mystic perceptions watching the flow and ebb of the resurrection spell while her physical eyes watched the increasingly one-sided battle of the dead in the valley to the southeast. Although the entire plan seemed strangely dishonorable to Eagle Woman—she preferred straightforward fighting to subterfuge and mysticism, although the humans' plan was quite intelligent and worthy of her husband's trickery—it was working well from what she could see.

Iktomi and the elders had clearly succeeded in their task. The breaking of the design sent a tremor through the folds of reality in every direction, and it had a salutary effect on the creatures in the human shells. Eagle Woman clearly saw their fear and discomfort at the design's destruction, and Caldwell, though still human and unquestionably dead, obviously gained something through his transformation, as he sensed the change as well. He motioned the dead to attack as soon as the design fell to White Hawk and his men.

The dead moved forward on Caldwell's command, and despite the warrior goddess' eons of battle experience, the sight of his army chilled Eagle Woman. When the plan was first discussed, the question of how to arm the dead was raised. The motivation behind an army of the resurrected was to minimize the possibility of death magic, but none of the Shoshone elders believed the soldiers would flee to a man; even in the face of death, soldiers are trained to fight on, and considering that the Tenth Cavalry was heavily armed and well-disciplined, simply sending the resurrected after them would not be enough.

"These are professional soldiers," Fights the Wind said. "They will fight, and they will fight well. Even an army of the dead has to be armed."

"If they're armed, they can kill," Aquinas responded, eyes blurred and watering from long hours of wood smoke. "Soldiers dying will add to the death magic in the air, and assist these…things in their overall plan."

"But if the design is down, how will they use it?" Fights the Wind asked.

"The energy will still be gathered," Aquinas said, "and if these things are necromancers, which I believe they are, they'll still be able to use it. The worldmaking Lieutenant Caldwell described won't work without the design, but who knows what else these things will be able to pull off, or drag into our world."

"Then we need to make sure the dead don't add to their numbers while defeating the living," said Calls Thunder Song, stroking his chin. "I have a thought."

Eagle Woman had smiled then, watching as Calls Thunder Song's ideas were put to good use. The first had been simple enough to do, especially as most of the dead were too far decayed or physically weak to do much damage: they simply made sure the dead carried no edged weapons. Of course, since many of the deceased were carrying knives, spears and other weapons at the time of death or burial, Aquinas and Fights the Wind were forced to check each resurrectee and make sure no blades were secreted upon their decaying persons. It wasn't a pleasant job. Aquinas was sick for an hour, and Fights the Wind claimed his sense of smell had yet to return, but they left a large pile of rusted and dirty weapons back in camp.

Rearming the dead with clubs and sticks seemed to have done the job, as far as Eagle Woman could see. While there were several soldiers downed, none were dead or mortally wounded, and the medicine women worked swiftly to make sure the worst injuries were tended as soon as possible. At worst, they suffered blows to the head or broken bones, and would be unconscious for a time. Many of the resurrectees grumbled at being ordered not to kill, but after a few of the first dead in the fray broke apart or disintegrated at the first blow struck, the sense of the order seemed to stick.

The second of Calls Thunder Song's ideas was yet more ingenious. "Most animals," the old shaman pointed out, "are deeply uncomfortable around things outside the natural order, horses more so than most." Why this was, no mortal exactly knew, but there it was. "Since the cavalry depends on horses for transport and attack, the resurrected army need simply direct their attention to the horses more than the humans riding them, and let natural instincts do the rest." Once the first stage of the spell was completed and the resurrected gathered at the valley several miles outside the Shoshone camp, the order went out: chase after the horses only. "Strike the soldiers at your leisure," Calls Thunder Song had told the assembled corpses, "but go for the horses first. They are your focus, my friends and brothers."

As Eagle Woman watched, the wisdom of the shaman's ideas turned clear. The first wave of the resurrected spooked soldiers and horses alike, but most of the soldiers were further back in the column, and couldn't clearly see the threat over the lip of the shallow valley. However, the horses, whose senses were more acute than their riders', were already primed to be fearful by the smell of death and the sense of otherness given off by the dead. Once the resurrected were in striking distance, they focused directly on the horses, which caused the mounts to rear, throwing the front lines into confusion and spreading panic through the formation faster than the humans could. Confused by the horses' behavior, the soldiers were ill-equipped for the appearance of hundreds of moving corpses, waving clubs and moaning with rage and fervor.

Despite her dislike for whites in general and the military in particular, Eagle Woman felt a grudging admiration for the discipline the soldiers showed. Even as their horses panicked and shattered their ordered formations in a mad attempt to flee, the cavalrymen worked to keep their mounts in line while defending themselves from the dead. Calls Thunder Song, however, understood what would happen better than she guessed. The dead, despite their rage and weapons, represented relatively little threat to a trained, healthy army. On the other hand, a thousand-pound bundle of muscle and flesh running amok with fear could overcome any ten soldiers, perhaps two or three times that number in a confined space. Multiply that horse by one or two hundred, Eagle Woman suddenly realized, and the shamans' plan could end up a victim of its own success. Men in blue uniforms were tossed in every direction as she watched, and it was only a matter of time before maddened hooves stomped a soldier's brains into the dirt.

Lieutenant, she sent to the leader of the resurrected, *have your army pull back. Soldiers being killed by their mounts will give just as much death energy to the darkness as those killed by your men.*

Understood, came the reply. *Pulling back now. We'll focus on breaking up the formation and scattering them.*

Eagle Woman nodded, though she knew Caldwell couldn't see her. *Human habit*, she noted, and wondered how her husband was doing. She sensed a flare from him when he worked his improvised plan on the Violet Falls bridge, and though she detected nothing since, she suspected Iktomi was lying low to keep the darkness off his scent. White Hawk, Mangas, and the surviving warriors were on their way back, though even if they rode their mounts to an exhausted death, they wouldn't get back before the battle was over, one way or the other.

Caldwell stood before Pineville and McAlister, the things responsible for so much death and darkness, and wondered – not for the first time since regaining his sanity – if they could truly be killed, if the death of their shells would end them as well or simply spill their substance forth and poison the world around them. He didn't want to hurt or endanger the soldiers arrayed against him. They were innocent of the purpose of their orders, and might not obey them if they knew. Still, the evil of the things walking as Pineville and Colonel McAlister was too great, too capable of horrible deeds to let live. He was evidence of that.

"Lieutenant, I'll enjoy tearing your soul from you," Pineville said. Its voice was muffled, the head hung at an awful angle upon its neck, but Caldwell was surprised to hear a wistful tone in Pineville's voice. "You really are exceptional livestock, but livestock you are."

"Amen," McAlister growled, blood caked upon its chin but otherwise visibly unharmed. Caldwell wasn't worried about the physical threat from Pineville. The shell could barely walk at more than a shuffle, and its balance was obviously affected by the broken neck. Still, McAlister presented a viable threat, and he knew either of them presented a mystical force he had no way to defend against or prevent. *Losing the design may have weakened them,* he thought, *but that could just make them more dangerous. Best raise the odds a little.*

McAlister approached first, its body crouched low in a fighting stance. Caldwell backed slowly to the lip of the valley, sensing the approach of a knot of resurrected up the low rise over the thrum of the shamans' and the magus's ongoing casting. He smiled mockingly at the colonel, waving him on, keeping his right hand back in a ready position. "Not much of a man in this world, are you, McAlister? Couldn't find the right size petticoat?"

The colonel said nothing, but its jaw tightened as it approached, eyes narrowing. Caldwell knew he'd scored a hit. "I remember you saying you'd wanted a female form here, but you made such a terrible man, I had a hard time telling the difference." Caldwell laughed loudly, taking his eyes purposefully off McAlister just for a moment, judging the distance between them at a glance.

Even suspecting an attack, the speed with which McAlister moved caught Caldwell by surprise. He dodged the first strike, but got a vicious kick to the ribs before he regained his balance. Caldwell stepped back, planting his back foot as he ducked under the roundhouse the enraged colonel threw. The lieutenant bent his knees, pulled McAlister to him, and heaved the surprised thing in the colonel's shell over the lip of the valley, straight into the knot of Shoshone and Kiowa corpses climbing the rise behind him. As Caldwell turned to face Pineville, he heard the thump of several bodies hitting the hard ground, and a chorus of enraged moans and howls as the dead found what appeared to be a real live cavalry officer in their midst. The solid strike of a club against bone was music to the lieutenant's ears. Caldwell saw a nearby medicine woman, wrapping a poultice around a slash in a young infantryman's arm and murmuring a healing spell, smile at the sound.

"I should never have killed you," Pineville said, its head flopping as it forced the words into the late morning air. "Death made you more determined."

"An apology?" Caldwell asked, moving slowly to the side. He'd wanted McAlister out of the way, but Pineville... Caldwell owed it a debt of pain and darkness. The lieutenant was eager to repay it.

"Admission of error," Pineville said, and launched himself at the lieutenant. *He may have been faking a little*, Caldwell thought as the Pineville shell hurtled toward him. *Good.*

The bodies crashed together and fell in a heap on the ground, tumbling into the dust as the dead scattered the living around them. Caldwell sprawled in the dirt, jagged rocks and clods scoring his face as Pineville ground his head down, shrieking and pounding its hands against him. Jackknifing onto his side, Caldwell pistoned an elbow into Pineville's chest, hearing a whoof of breath escape the blocked throat. It was a satisfying sound. Caldwell repeated the action twice more, feeling more than hearing ribs flex and crack under the blows. He quickly rolled to the left, overturning Pineville's body and sending it sprawling. Gaining his feet, he soundly kicked Pineville's ribs three times in succession, now hearing the splinter of bone loud in the air. He shouted with manic joy, and lifted his foot to stomp on the thing's skull.

Pineville rolled suddenly, raised its hand, and shouted something raw and jagged. A blinding gout of flame shot from its hand and into Caldwell's face. He turned his head instantly, but the left side of his face was engulfed in eldritch flame, blinding him in that eye and filling the air with the stench of charred meat. Caldwell staggered to the side, and Pineville swept his legs out from under him with a ragged but effective kick. Screaming hoarsely, the thing in Pineville's skin leapt upon Caldwell's stunned form and clawed at his chest, shredding his uniform within moments and digging into the rigored flesh beneath it. A memory of his resurrection surfaced, clouded in blood and bone-deep agony, and Caldwell knew Pineville was trying to undo his resurrection. For a moment, the lieutenant considered letting the thing complete its spell, considered letting it end his undead existence and send him into a peaceful oblivion.

The moment passed, and Caldwell smiled up at the thing, a crazed grin that gave it pause.

"Should have dug in a little quicker," Caldwell said, and grabbing the front of Pineville's shirt, bucked his body and rolled sharply to the side, reversing their positions. Still holding onto the shirt, Caldwell began pummeling Pineville's face and chest, powerful blows that crunched bone and cartilage, spattering blood and spittle in all directions. In moments, Pineville's face was a morass of blood and bruise, its chest a jagged mass of torn, splintered flesh. The lieutenant punched the thing's throat repeatedly, shattering the larynx and esophagus beyond even magical healing, and then stopped for a moment, looking down at Pineville's ruined body.

"I admit, I'm curious," Caldwell said, his voice rough and unrecognizable in his ears. "Just what the hell is inside this meat?"

Although Caldwell saw no expression on Pineville's ruined face – could make nothing out of the bloodied ruin – he felt sure the shaking of the battered head and the scrabbling at his chest meant Pineville didn't want him to find out. This, the lieutenant thought, was an excellent reason to explore further.

"Capital idea, Mr. Pineville, thank you," said Caldwell. His right hand rose, clenched into a fist. Taking all the pain of his death and resurrection, the shame of being used in the murders of many innocents aboard the train, and the raw hatred he felt against these degenerate beings that dared to attempt genocide against his world, Caldwell focused that energy and drove his fist through Pineville's chest, into the obsidian miasma of its being.

The thing that, even now, thought of itself as Pineville screamed, a spirit-curdling wail of agony and lost dreams as Caldwell's hand blasted through the flesh it inhabited for so long and into the fluidic substance of its true self. Unable to bear the touch of unaltered reality, it squirmed and sought to escape from Caldwell, who would not be denied. He grabbed Pineville's heaving chest and tore the cavity wide open, exposing the blackness within to the sun's immolating touch. Pineville screamed again, the sound flying past human registers and into the psionic, an agonized howl sensed for miles. Caldwell, with both hands, reached into the cavity and pulled the thing's true being, riven of the First's flesh and exposed to human reality, out into the blazing morning light. Between the uncontrolled influx of necromantic energy and the destructive blast of the sun, the thing called Pineville had only an instant to think of home, to plead across universes for mercy from the First for its abject failure.

Forgive me, First--, the thing disguised as Aldous Pineville prayed in its last moments, and like a thunderbolt, or the horrible attention of the Eye, the response from beyond the edge of existence rolled into its disintegrating mind:

/no/

For the second time that day, the sun rose over the prairie, blinding light and heat unleashed in a thanatopic maelstrom. The sound of gods clapping, or something immense falling, blasted over the valley, bowling over the living and the dead. When it faded, and the battlefield was visible again, a roughly circular area of the prairie, about ten feet in diameter, had been scoured clean to the bedrock beneath. Of the two beings that battled in the center of the sterile region, there was no sign, no trace of either the thing from another realm or the brave lieutenant who fought and vanquished it, even into a second death.

Chapter 22

High overhead, the noontime sun blazed hard and furious on the prairie, raising the heat and stench on the wind to nauseous levels. Between the stampeding of terrified horses, many of which were frightened into frothing seizures, the panic among the soldiers at facing an army of corpses and the rising tide of decay from the dead, the battle was a wholehearted rout. Several soldiers were severely wounded from being battered by the dead, and their own mounts, but the Shoshone medicine women were quick and wise in their applications, and no one succumbed to death.

By mid-afternoon, the battle was completed. All but one or two of the soldiers were accounted for, and those not in custody had long since retreated as fast as booted feet or recaptured mounts could take them. Although Eagle Woman's sense told her something was left incomplete, she saw no reason to continue the service of the marching dead, and approached the mystic circle with the magus and the two shamans. There had been no increase of necromantic energy since the massive discharge that destroyed the alien Pineville and the brave lieutenant, and the fight seemed finished.

"It is finished," she called as she approached, her steps soft as she scanned the area for whatever nagged at her perception. *Together*, she thought, *we can address what is wrong after laying the faithful dead back to rest.*

None of the men in the circle saw her, their eyes closed in mystic concentration, but they nodded in unison, and the spell working took a slower rhythm as they ended the chanting, winding down the casting gradually. Slowly, the brilliant emerald aura faded around them, and the sensation of massive power held in check dialed down to a background hum. Soon it disappeared altogether, and the men slumped inside the circle, drained and pale but unhurt.

Aquinas opened his eyes first, smiling as he saw Eagle Woman's curved form beyond the circle's edge. She saw his mouth start to move, and in the instant before the first word sounded, his attention shifted to something behind her, and to her surprise, her first sensation was relief. Whatever caught her senses, warned her of a nagging problem, was coming to pass and could be addressed. Faster than thought, she whirled to face whatever was behind her.

The dead weren't kind to the colonel, she immediately saw. Its uniform was in tatters, the jacket stripped from its frame, the shirt barely more than bloodstained sleeves and a ragged sash across its scarred chest. A blunt gash across its forehead showed greasy bone, and a checkerboard of blood spatters coated it from head to toe in a clotted rainbow of red and black. At some point, a club struck it in the eye socket, cracking skull and rupturing the eyeball into a weeping trail down its cheek. The creature within had patched its shell with reckless drafts of thanatopic energy, which sparkled and burned in a dozen places on its body, most brightly in the empty eye socket, now shining a malevolent indigo. Eagle Woman wasn't fooled by the creature's battered appearance: its aura was deranged but fiery with power. McAlister would not perish without a fight, or easily.

The creature that called itself colonel howled something brutish and caustic, the closest its ruined throat could come to its native language. Eagle Woman smiled grimly. Regardless of its power, the creature faced a warrior goddess now. She gestured sharply at the exhausted men now behind her to stand down; after such an involved casting, she was sure they didn't have the magical energy or physical strength to continue, and other challenges might still arise this day. This was her fight.

"I hope that was a challenge," she said in the mother tongue, older than the stars and the void in-between, "because I'm going to answer it."

The colonel howled again and charged, still lightning fast despite its wounds. Eagle Woman ducked and rolled, coming to her feet and spinning to face the colonel again in one smooth motion. She cast a hunting glamour at the same moment McAlister threw a coiled ball of venomous light, and the poison burst harmlessly against the illusion, destroying both. Darting in, she swiped at the colonel's face, scoring its cheek to the enamel of its molars and spraying black blood in a jet. McAlister snarled and swung its hand in a short arc, catching Eagle Woman in the ribs with the flat of its hand. The impact threw her several feet; a mortal would have felt jagged bone pierce their lungs, but she merely felt the breath whistle from her lungs for a moment.

As she rolled, she slammed her hand palm down upon the ground, casting a quick elemental spell she recalled from one of Iktomi's wilder escapades. Thunder rolled in the earth and rocks sprang forth in a jagged bolt line from her hand. The colonel lost its footing on one, tumbling to earth heavily and bouncing its damaged face off an upthrust stone. Hissing with rage, it leapt to its feet, only to receive a punch like a mule's kick in the mouth. Shattered teeth flew in a bloody nimbus around its head. As it fell, it spat a word at her, which gained substance in the air and came to earth as black fire. It touched down and spread like its mortal cousin, but everything it touched withered with age and fell to dust within moments, and it arrowed along the ground, straight toward Eagle Woman.

She leapt backward, turning in the air and landing on her feet facing the onrushing fire. A bolt of electric fury slowed its advance but did not stop it, so Eagle Woman moved swiftly to the side and cast a harvest spell at it, counterpointing the entropic spell with a life enchantment. Although the spell stopped the black fire for a moment, creating a swirling globe of green and black energy, the black fire won out, swallowing the enchantment whole and resuming its course toward Eagle Woman.

McAlister laughed hoarsely, its words mumbled through a shattered jaw and jagged teeth. "What will you do now, warrior goddess? Even you will fall to entropy one day."

The fire darted toward Eagle Woman, who saw an opening and dived past it, springing to her feet near McAlister. Without conscious thought, she snaked out a powerful arm and grabbed McAlister by the neck, snatching it off its feet with one mighty pull. Smoothly lifting it clear of the ground, she held it over her head and waited for a second, letting the black fire draw closer to her feet. Faster than thought, the entropic charge covered the ground between them and leapt at her, but Eagle Woman was faster yet, and she threw McAlister at the black fire.

McAlister and the black fire met in midair, entwining around each other like lovers and falling to earth. The colonel let out a whistling scream and roared several barked syllables, slowing the progression of the fire but not stopping it. Pieces of the shell that was once Hamish McAlister dissolved and reformed as Eagle Woman watched the battle, and although the thing beneath the colonel's skin was pernicious and determined, she quickly saw it was losing the fight. Belatedly, the thought occurred to her that she did not know if the black fire would stop when it finished with the colonel. It howled a longer series of enraged words to no effect as she watched, and she recalled the massive discharge of energy Pineville's destruction caused.

"Shit," she said in the mother tongue.

Not yet, a familiar voice said in her head. *I have an idea.*

Eagle Woman turned to Aquinas as his words tumbled into her mind, explaining what he intended to do. His plan had the virtue of being simple, but that was almost the total of its virtues. Opening a portal in the dreaming and throwing the entropically infected McAlister in would save the human world, but unless they had a destination in mind, the discharge of energy might just destroy the dreaming, and any worlds not yet closed to it, such as the High Prairies. She explained this to him in a burst of images, and added, not unkindly, *You have half an idea. Where will you send it?*

Isn't it obvious, an even more familiar voice chimed in. *I believe the whites even have a term for this type of movement: return to sender.*

Eagle Woman felt the tiniest touch on her hand, a pressure she'd half-believed she'd never feel again. She looked down to see a tiny red and yellow striped spider, white lightning jags on his abdomen, stroking her skin, minuscule eyes flashing mischievously.

"Your timing is still unsurpassed, husband," she smiled, a warm relief rushing through her. "You know which realm this thing belongs to?"

I know the address, yes. The monstrosity fairly shouts it from its being, came the reply.

And I have a portal spell ready to take it there, Aquinas thought to them both.

"Let's send this thing home," Eagle Woman said, and as a parting gift, cast a small but potent hex on the writhing colonel. It would not take effect right away, she reflected, and should the black fire win, might not take effect at all. That was a chance she was willing to take.

Aquinas, standing shakily but upright, cast a complex two-handed runesign and opened his hands, just as Iktomi had taught him before the day's work began. A slab of darkness appeared before him; not the blackness of the infested dreaming, but the infinite ebon of a realm where all life was corrupted and all angles were skewed, the acheronian shade of McAlister's home world. Aquinas only caught a glimpse of what lay within—angles that caused the eyes pain, colors that sickened the mind, monstrous flesh—but a glimpse was enough. He turned his face aside and yelled, "Cast it in, now!"

A flicker of will from Eagle Woman, and the nearly devoured colonel shot through the hole in the world. Once the thing and its entropic spell were safely through the portal, Aquinas released the casting, and the portal flickered into nothingness. Unnoticed by anyone, even Eagle Woman, Iktomi sent a last-second adjustment to the portal spell, altering the infinitely complex coordinates of the portal casting by just a fraction here, a minute decimal there. The spider god smiled at his mischief, and set about returning to human form in order to more properly greet his friends.

In the tallest spire of the First's temple, between the calcified agony walls and the cancerous miasma pumps, sits the Vestibule of the Eye, the place where the concentrated miasma of the First's purified flesh rests between manifestations as the Eye. Here, It greets supplicants, devours the flesh of the devout and the souls of the unworthy, and plots the metastasis of all within Its gargantuan appetite. Pulsing with miasmic energy, It waits for the way to open to a new realm, modified to accept its cells and filled with braying, bleeding cattle.

As It waits, a portal appears before It, a darkness as black as space but somehow warmer than Its own. Even faster than Its own thought, the portal disgorges a writhing ball of flailing flesh and black fire into Its presence and closes, sealing the way behind forever. Stunned by the portal's flash of existence, It nevertheless examines the flesh before it and senses the entity that in the human world was called McAlister. The black fire is of no consequence to It, but the McAlister thing knew it was not to return before the way was opened, and It will have answers before ending the failure's line and sucking the marrow of McAlister's soul for Its pleasure.

/the way is not opened. explain this/

McAlister tries to scream a warning, thinks loudly, *Send me elsewhere, First. You face a trap!* Fortunately, Eagle Woman's hex against McAlister communicating holds, in part because of McAlister's attempt to increase its energy stores using the recently generated thanatopic energy. As McAlister would have gladly told the First, it was now a supercharged energy bomb being rapidly devoured by the black fire. And, as Iktomi was delighted to discover, such energy was a fundamental force in the First's realm, so a sudden discharge of this energy in that universe would have far greater effect than in the human reality.

/speak quickly, i grow hungry/

Release me! McAlister cried to no avail.

The black fire finished its meal of the human shell. It touched the miasmic being within, and formed a bridge between the thanatopic energy and the entropic reaction to the fluid inside. Had the miasmic beings ever conceived of a doomsday weapon to be used against themselves or their god, it would have taken a form much like McAlister in the last instants of its life.

/**what is--**/

Across the realm of the First, a new sun dawned, bright and terrible in the infinite night.

Epilogue

Outside the lodge of the shaman Calls Thunder Song, near the hunting grounds for the Shoshone tribe for the last several centuries, two gods sat on the hard prairie floor, watching the sun set slowly in an explosion of red and gold clouds. Neither had said much since the victory over the alien entities from another realm just a few scant hours before. The days leading up to the battle were exhausting, and even the gods get tired.

Although battling darkness and crazed meat suits was tiring, their exhaustion was negligible compared to the white magus and the shamans, who worked themselves almost to the High Prairies without any help from Coyote. Thus, the gods, who are more merciful than their tales sometimes suggest, consented to stand guard over the last of the day while the magus and the shamans slept within.

Iktomi sat against the rough lodge walls, eyes closed as he contemplated the future of humanity and the gods. Despite the resounding defeat of the things from beyond space, mostly due to the valor of the humans, the Spirit Councils decided to continue with the severing of the High Prairies from the human realm, leaving only a small path for the souls of the dead to pass through. How Coyote intended to enforce that was an issue Iktomi was very interested in, but the upshot of the decree was simple. Either Iktomi could leave the human realm behind forever, or he could forsake the High Prairies for all eternity. Neither option appealed to the spider god, but his answer depended much on Eagle Woman's answer.

The spider god reached out his hand, once again clothed as a Negro porter (how he loved that look, for reasons he couldn't quite explain), and touched the hand of his once, and he hoped future, wife. Her eyes did not turn from the sunset, but she smiled dreamily, almost softly, at his touch. "Yes, husband, I am still thinking it over."

"No hurry. Coyote did give us until moonrise to decide where eternity will be spent, after all." Iktomi yawned once, an exhalation smelling faintly of garlic and cinnamon. "I love this mortal realm, and would hate to miss out on everything to come, but the High Prairies are home. Giving either up is preposterous."

"Mmm," Eagle Woman said. "The change you love is what the Spirit Councils fear. Our people haven't yet adapted to the white ways."

"Those who could pass through the dreaming never will adapt," Iktomi said. "The ones who can't...well, either they will, or they won't. I feel obligated to stay for them, but on the other hand, they'll forget us in time. They must, for survival's sake."

"Maybe," Eagle Woman said. "Migrations have already begun. In a few days, the remaining few will begin to turn away from the old ways, adapting to this new world."

"Or dying," Iktomi said.

"Either way," Eagle Woman replied, "our time as we were is ending, but new things come. Change is not outside our grasp."

"That sounds...optimistic, for you," Iktomi said, turning to look at his love in the day's fading glory. "What brings that on?"

Eagle Woman smiled again, all traces of the blade gone from her visage for a pure, sweet instant. Iktomi remembered that look from eons past, and a sudden suspicion struck him.

He put a gentle hand on her stomach, sensing the energy flow within, and grinned wildly. "You minx! Have you told the magus?"

The warrior goddess laughed loudly, tickled Iktomi wasn't angry. "No, and I may not. It was a function of necessity, not a betrothal or any such foolishness. What happened… was right, then and for the future."

Iktomi nodded soberly. He saw her decision was never really in doubt, and thus, neither was his. Looking forward, he saw how the world would change and unfold, the turns and ripples he and Eagle Woman would face, alone and with others not yet born. A smile spread across his face as he contemplated the changes to come. He couldn't wait to break the news to Coyote. *Won't he be pissed*, Iktomi the spider god thought, and laughed joyously, his hand holding Eagle Woman's tightly as they watched the night steal closer.

Acknowledgments

If it takes a village to raise a child, it takes a small nation to create a book. Listing everyone who had a hand in this labor of love you're holding or who helped me along the way would require, at the least, another chapter, but I can at least get the big names out of the way. The good folks at Montag Press deserve a round of thanks, particularly Mara Hodges, whose suggestions and editorial eye saved this author from a metric ton of gaffes and embarrassments. If you find more, those are on me. Before I ever worked up the nerve to submit *Iron and Smoke* to a publisher, my friend and former roommate Charles Bingham provided beta reading services and encouragement, which helped more than I might have let on (thanks, Bingo). Finally, while my immediate and extended family have never been anything less than supportive, special thanks go to my wife Paige, who constantly, lovingly nagged me to get my ass in gear and get published.

About the author

Brandon Nolta is a writer, editor, and professional curmudgeon living in the transportation-challenged wilds of north Idaho. After earning an MFA, he went slightly mad. Nothing much happened with that, so he gave it up and started working for respectable companies again, which he still does when he's not pounding away at the keyboard to the sweet strains of Miles Davis and the occasional burst of EDM. His fiction and poetry have appeared in *Stupefying Stories, The Pedestal Magazine, Every Day Fiction, Perihelion, Strong Verse,* and a cacophony of other publications. *Iron and Smoke* is his first novel; he has yet to admit to a second.